William Morris, Joseph Jacobs

Old French Romances

William Morris, Joseph Jacobs

Old French Romances

ISBN/EAN: 9783337049102

Printed in Europe, USA, Canada, Australia, Japan

Cover: Foto ©Andreas Hilbeck / pixelio.de

More available books at **www.hansebooks.com**

OLD FRENCH
ROMANCES

DONE INTO ENGLISH

BY

WILLIAM MORRIS

WITH AN INTRODUCTION BY

JOSEPH JACOBS

LONDON
GEORGE ALLEN, RUSKIN HOUSE
1896

Printed by BALLANTYNE, HANSON & Co.
At the Ballantyne Press

INTRODUCTION

M ANY of us have first found our way into the Realm of Romance, properly so called, through the pages of a little crimson clad volume or the *Bibliothèque Elzevirienne.** Its last pages contain the charming Cante-Fable of *Aucassin et Nicolete*, which Mr. Walter Pater's praises and Mr. Andrew Lang's brilliant version have made familiar to all lovers of letters. But the same volume contains four other tales, equally charming in their way, which Mr. William Morris has now made part of English literature by writing them out again for us in English, reproducing, as his alone can do of living men's, the tone, the colour, the charm of the Middle Ages. His versions have appeared in three successive issues of the Kelmscott Press, which

* *Nouvelles françaises en prose du xiii*ième *siècle*, par MM. L. Moland et C. D'Hericault. (Paris : Janet, 1856.)

have been eagerly snapped up by the lovers of good books. It seemed a pity that these cameos of romance should suffer the same fate as Mr. Lang's version of *Aucassin et Nicolete*, which has been swept off the face of the earth by the Charge of the Six Hundred, who were lucky enough to obtain copies of the only edition of that little masterpiece of translation. Mr. Morris has, therefore, consented to allow his versions of the Romances to be combined into one volume in a form not unworthy of their excellence but more accessible to those lovers of books whose purses have a habit of varying in inverse proportion to the amount of their love. He has honoured me by asking me to introduce them to that wider public to which they now make their appeal.

I

ALMOST all literary roads lead back to Greece. Obscure as still remains the origin of that *genre* of romance to which the tales before us belong, there is little doubt that their models, if not their originals, were once extant at Constantinople. Though in no single instance has the Greek original been discovered of any of these romances, the mere name of their heroes would be in most cases sufficient to prove their Hellenic or Byzantine origin. Heracles, Athis, Porphirias, Parthenopeus, Hippomedon, Protesilaus, Cliges, Cleomades, Clarus, Berinus —names such as these can come but from one quarter of Europe, and it is as easy to guess how and when they came as whence. The first two crusades brought the flower of European chivalry to Constantinople and restored that spiritual union between Eastern and Western Christendom that had been interrupted by the great schism of the Greek and Roman Churches. The crusaders

Introduction came mostly from the Lands of Romance. Permanent bonds of culture began to be formed between the extreme East and the extreme West of Europe by intermarriage, by commerce, by the admission of the nobles of Byzantium within the orders of chivalry. These ties went on increasing throughout the twelfth century till they culminated at its close with the foundation of the Latin kingdom of Constantinople. In European literature these historic events are represented by the class of romances represented in this volume, which all trace back to versions in verse of the twelfth century, though they were done into prose somewhere in Picardy during the course of the next century. Daphnis and Chloe, one might say, had revived after a sleep of 700 years, and donned the garb and spoke the tongue of Romance.

II

The very first of our tales illustrates admirably the general course of their history. It is, in effect, a folk etymology of the name of the great capital of the Eastern Empire. Constantinople, so runs the tale, received that name instead of Byzantium, because of the remarkable career of one of its former rulers, Coustans. M. Wesselovsky has published in *Romania* (vi. l. seq.) the *Introduction Dit de l'empereur Constant*, the verse original of the story before us, and in this occur the lines—

Pour ce que si *nobles* estoit
Et que nobles œvres faisoit
L'appielloient *Constant le noble*
Et pour çou ot *Constantinnoble*
Li cytés de Bissence a non.

From which it would appear that we are mistaken in thinking of the capital of Turkey as the " City of Constantine," whereas it is rather Constant the Noble, and the name Coustant is further explained as " costing " too much. Constantinople, therefore, is the city that costs too much, according to the prophetic etymology of the folk.

The only historic personage with whom this Coustant can be identified is Constantius Chlorus, the father of Constantine the Great and the husband of St. Helena, to whom legend ascribes the discovery of the Holy Rood. But the Coustans of our story never lived or ruled on land or sea, and his predecessor, Muselinus, is altogether unknown to Byzantine annals, while their interlaced history reads more like a page of the *Arabian Nights* than of Gibbon.

ix

Introduction   But such a legend could scarcely have arisen elsewhere than at Constantinople. It is one of those fables that the disinherited folk have at all times invented to solace themselves for their disinherison. The sudden and fated rise of one of the folk to the heights of power occurs sufficiently often to afford material for the day dreams of ambitious youth. There is even a popular tendency to attribute a lowly origin to all favourites of fortune, as witness the legends that have grown up about the early careers of Beckett, Whittington, Wolsey, none of whom was as ill-born as popular tradition asserts. Yet such legends invariably grow up in the country of their heroes, which is the only one sufficiently interested in their career, so far as the common people are concerned. Hence the very nature of our story would cause us to locate its origin on the banks of the Bosphorus.

But once originated in this manner, there is no limit to the travels it may take. Curiously enough, the very legend before us in all its details has found a home among the English peasantry. The Rev. S. Baring-Gould collected in Yorkshire a story which he contributed to Henderson's *Folklore of the Northern Counties*,

x

and entitled *The Fish and the Ring.** legend a girl comes as the unwelcome sixth of the family of a very poor man who lived under the shadow of York Minster. A Knight, riding by on the day of her birth, discovers, by consultation of the Book of Fate, that she was destined to marry his son. He offers to adopt her, and throws her into the River Ouse. A fisherman saves her, and she is again discovered after many years by the Knight, who learns what Fate has still in store for his son. He sends her to his brother at Scarborough with a fatal letter, ordering him to put her to death. But on the way she is seized by a band of robbers, who read the letter and replace it by one ordering the Baron's son to be married to her immediately on her arrival.

When the Baron discovers that he has not been able to evade the decree of fate he still persists in his persecution, and taking a ring from his finger throws it into the sea, saying that the girl shall never live with his son till she can show him that ring. She wanders about and becomes a scullery-maid at a great castle, and one day

* I have given a version of it in my *English Fairy Tales*, and there is a ballad on the subject entitled *The Cruel Knight*.

xi

the letter, "On delivery, please kill bearer," is scarcely likely to have occurred twice to the popular imagination, and one is almost brought to the conclusion that the romance before us was itself either directly or indirectly the source of all the European Folk-tales in which the letter "To kill bearer" occurs. And as we have before traced the Romance back to Constantinople, one is further tempted to trace back the Letter itself to a reminiscence of Homer's σήματα λυγρά.

I have said above that no Greek original of any of these Romances has hitherto been discovered. But in the case of King Coustans we can at any rate get within appreciable distance of it. As recently as 1895 a learned Teuton, Dr. Ernst Kuhn, pointed out, appropriately enough in the *Byzantinische Zeitschrift*, the existence of an Ethiopic and of an Arabic version of the legend. He found in one of Mr. Quaritch's catalogues a description of an illuminated Ethiopic MS., once belonging to King Theodore of Magdala fame, which from the account given of several of the illustrations he was enabled to identify as the story of "The Man born to be King." His name in the Ethiopic version is Thalassion, or Ethiopic words to that effect, and

Introduction the Greek *provenance* of the story is thereby established. Dr. Kuhn was also successful in finding an Arabic version done by a Coptic Christian. In both these versions the story is told as a miracle due to the interference of the Angel Michael ; and it is a curious coincidence that in Mr. Morris' poetical version of our story in the " Earthly Paradise" he calls his hero Michael. Unless some steps are taken to prevent the misunderstanding, it is probable that some Teutonic investigator of the next century will, on the strength of this identity of names, bring Mr. Morris in guilty of a knowledge of Ethiopic.

But for the name of the hero one might have suspected these Oriental versions of being derived, not from a Greek, but from an Indian original. Mr. Tawney has described a variant found in the *Kathākosa* * which resembles our tale much more closely than any of the European folk-tales in the interesting point that the predestined bride herself finds the fatal letter and makes the satisfactory substitution. In the Indian tale this is done with considerable ingenuity and *vraisemblance*. The girl's name is Visha, and the operative clause of the fatal letter is :

* See Clouston, *Book of Sindibad*, p. 279.

" Before this man has washed his feet, do thou
with speed
Give him poison (*visham*), and free my heart
from care."

The lady thinks (or wishes) that her father is a
bad orthographist, and corrects his spelling by
omitting the final *m*, so that the letter reads :
" Give him Visha," with results more satisfactory
to the young lady than to her father. This
variant is so very close to our tale, while the
letter incident in it is so much more naturally
developed than in the romance that one might
almost suspect it of having been the original.
But we must know more about the *Kathākosa* and
about the communication between Byzantium
and India before we can decisively determine
which came first.

III

Amis and Amil were the David and Jonathan,
the Orestes and Pylades, of the mediæval world.
Dr. Hofmann, who has edited the earliest French
verse account of the Legend, enumerates nearly
thirty other versions of it in almost all the
tongues of Western and Northern Europe, not
to mention various versions which have crept
into different collections of the Lives of the

Saints. For their peerless friendship raised them to the ranks of the martyrs, at any rate, at Mortara and Novara, where, according to the Legend, they died. The earliest of all these forms is a set of Latin Hexameters by one Radulfus Tortarius, born at Fleury, 1063, lived in Normandy, and died some time after 1122. It was, therefore, possible that the story had come back with the first crusaders, and the Grimms attribute to it a Greek original. But in its earliest as well as in its present form, it is definitely located on Romance soil, while the names of the heroes are clearly Latin (Amicus and Æmilius). It was, however, only at a later stage that the story was affiliated to the Epic Cycle of Charlemagne. On the face of it there is clearly stamped the impress of popular tradition. Heads are not so easily replaced, except by a freak of the Folk imagination. It is probably for this reason that M. Gaston Paris attributes an Oriental origin to the latter part of the tale, and for the same reason the Benedictine Fathers have had serious doubts about admitting it into the *Acta Sanctorum.* On the other hand, the editors of the French text, the translation of which we have before us, go so far as to conjecture that there is a historic germ for the whole

xvi

Legend in certain incidents of the War of Charlemagne against Didier. But as the whole connection of the Legend with the Charlemagne Cycle
is late, we need not attribute much importance to,
indeed, we may at once dismiss their conjecture.

These disputes of the pundits cannot destroy
the charm of the Legend. Never, even in
antiquity, have the claims of friendship been
urged with such a passionate emphasis. The
very resemblance of the two heroes is symbolic
of their similarity of character ; the very name
of one of them is Friend pure and simple. The
world is well lost for friendship's sake on the
one side, on the other nearest and dearest are
willingly and literally sacrificed on the altar of
friendship. One of the most charming of the
Fioretti tells how St. Francis overcame in himself the mediæval dread at the touch of a leper,
and washed and tended one of the poor unfortu-
nates. He was but following the example ot
Amil, who was not deterred by the dreaded
sound of the " tartavelle "—the clapper or rattle
which announced the approach of the leper*—
from tending his friend.

* Figured in M. Ulysse Robert, *Signes d'infamie au
moyen âge*, Paris, 1891. Lovers of Stevenson will re-
member the effective use made of this in *The
Black Arrow.*

Here again romance has points of contact with the folk tale. The end of the Grimms' tale of *Faithful John* is clearly the same as that of *Amis and Amile*.* Once more we are led to believe in some dependence of the Folk-Tale on Romance, or, *vice versâ*, since an incident like that of resuscitation by the sacrifice of a child is not likely to occur independently to two different tellers of tales. The tale also contains the curious incident of the unsheathed sword in bed, which, both in romances and folk-tales, is regarded as a complete bar to any divorce court proceedings. It is probable that the sword was considered as a living person, so that the principle *ne coram publico* was applied, and the sword was regarded as a kind of chaperon.† It is noteworthy that the incident occurs in *Aladdin and the Wonderful Lamp*, which is a late interpolation into the *Arabian Nights*, and may be due there to

* It has been suggested that the names of our heroes have given rise to the proverbial saying : "A miss (Amis) is as good as a mile (Amile)," but notwithstanding the high authority from which the suggestion emanates, it is little more than a pun.

† For occurrences of this incident in sagas, etc., see Grimm, *Deutsche Rechtsalterthümer*, 168–70 ; in folk-tales, Dasent, *Tales from the Norse*, cxxxiv.–v., *n.*

xviii

European influence. But another incident in the *Introduction* romance suggests that it was derived from a folk-tale rather than the reverse. The two bowls of wood given to the heroes at baptism are clearly a modification of that familiar incident in folk-tales, where one of a pair leaves with the other a " Lifetoken " * which will sympathetically indicate his state of health. As this has been considerably attenuated in our romance, we are led to the conclusion that it is itself an adaptation of a folk-tale.

IV

The tale of *King Florus*—the gem of the book—recalls the early part of Shakespeare's *Cymbeline* and the bet about a wife's virtue, which forms the subject of many romances, not a few folk-tales, and at least one folk-song. *The Romance of the Violet*, by Gerbert de Montruil, *circa* 1225, derives its name from the mother's mark of the heroine, which causes her husband to lose his bet. This was probably the source of Boccaccio's novel (ii. 9), from which Shakespeare's more immediately grew.

* Mr. Hartland has studied the " Lifetoken " in the eighth chapter of his elaborate treatise on the Legend of Perseus.

The Gaelic version of this incident, collected by Campbell (*The Chest*, No. 14), is clearly not of folk origin, but derived directly or indirectly from Boccaccio, in whom alone the Chest is found. Yet it is curious that, practically, the same story as the *Romance of the Violet* is found among folk-songs in modern Greece and in Modern Scotland. In Passow's collection of Romaic Folk Songs there is one entitled *Maurianos and the King*, which is in substance our story ; and it is probably the existence of this folk-song which causes M. Gaston Paris to place our tale among the romances derived from Byzantium. Yet Motherwell in his *Minstrelsy* has a ballad entitled *Reedisdale and Wise William*, which has the bet as its motive. Here again, then, we have a connection between our romance and the story-store of European folk, and at the same time some slight link with Byzantium.

V

The tale of "Oversea" has immediate connection with the Crusades, since its heroine is represented to be no other than the great grandmother of Saladin. But her adventures resemble those of Boccaccio's Princess of Babylon (ii. 7),

xx

who was herself taken from one of the Greek *Introduction* romances by Xenophon of Ephesus. Here again, then, we can trace back to Greek influence reaching Western Europe in the twelfth century through the medium of the Crusades. But the tale finds no echo among the folk, so far as I am aware, and is thus purely and simply a romance of adventure.

This, however, is not the only story connected with the Crusades in which the Soudan loves a lady of the Franks. Saladin is credited by the chatty Chronicle of Rheims with having gained the love of Eleanor, wife of Louis VII., when they were in Palestine on the Second Crusade. As Saladin did not ascend the throne till twenty years later, chronology is enabled to clear his memory of this piece of scandal. But its existence chimes in with such relations between Moslem and Christian as is represented in our story, which were clearly not regarded at the time with any particular aversion by the folk; they agree with Cardinal Mazarin on this point.

So much for the origin of our tales. Yet who cares for origins nowadays? We are all democrats now, and a tale, like a man, is welcomed for its merits and not for its pedigree. Yet even democracy must own, that pedigree often leaves its trace in style and manner, and certainly the tales before us owe some of their charm to their lineage. "Out of Byzantium by Old France" is a good strain by which to produce thoroughbred romance.

Certainly we breathe the very air of romance in these stories. There is none of your modern priggish care for the state of your soul. Men take rank according to their might, women are valued for their beauty alone. Adventures are to the adventurous, and the world is full of them. Every place but that in which one is born is equally strange and wondrous. Once beyond the bounds of the city walls and none knows what may happen. We have stepped forth into the Land of Faerie, but at least we are in the open air.

Mr. Pater seems to regard our stories as being a premonition of the freedom and gaiety of the Renaissance rather than as especially characteristic of the times of Romance. All that one need remark upon such misconception is that it only proves that Mr. Pater knew less of Romance Literature than he did of his favourite subject. The freshness, the gaiety, the direct outlook into life are peculiar neither to Romance nor Renaissance; their real source was the *esprit Gaulois*. But the unquestioning, if somewhat external, piety, the immutability of the caste system, the spirit of adventure, the frankly physical love of woman, the large childlike wonder, these are of the essence of Romance, and they are fully represented in the tales before us. Wonder and reverence, are not these the parents of Romance? Intelligent curiosity and intellectual doubt—those are what the Renaissance brought. Without indulging in invidious comparisons between the relative value of these gifts, I would turn back to our stories with the remark that much of the wonder which they exhibit is due to the vague localisation which runs through them. Rome, Paris, Byzantium, form spots of light on the mediæval map, but all between is in the dim obscure where anything may occur, and the brave man moves about with his life in his hands.

We thus obtain that absence of localisation

Introduction which helps to give the characteristic tone to mediæval romance. Events happen in a sort of sublime No Man's Land. They happen, as it were, at the root of the mountains, on the glittering plain, and in short, we get news from Nowhere. It seems, therefore, peculiarly appropriate that they should be done into English in the same style and by the same hand that has already written the annals of those countries of romance. Writing here, in front of Mr. Morris's versions, I am speaking, as it were, before his face, and must not say all that I should like in praise of the style in which he has clothed them, and of its appropriateness for its present purpose. I should merely like to recall the fact that it was used by him in his versions of the Sagas as long ago as 1869. Since then it has been adopted by all who desire to give an appropriate English dress to their versions of classic or mediæval masterpieces of a romantic character. We may take it, I think, that this style has established itself as the only one suitable for a romantic version, and who shall use it with ease and grace if not its original inventor ?

If their style suits Mr. Morris, there is little doubt that their subject is equally congenial. I cannot claim to be in his confidence on the

xxiv

point, but it is not difficult, I fancy, to guess what has attracted him to them. Nearly all of them, we have seen, are on the borderland between folk-tale and romance. It is tales such as these that Mr. Morris wishes to see told in tapestry on the walls of the Moot-Hall of the Hammersmith of Nowhere. It was by tales such as these that he first won a hearing from all lovers of English literature. The story of Jason is but a Greek setting of a folk-tale known among the Gaels as the *Battle of the Birds*, and in Norse as the *Master Maid*. Many of the tales which the travellers told one another in the *Earthly Paradise*, such as *The Man born to be King* (itself derived from the first of our stories), *The Land East of the Sun and West of the Moon*, and *The Ring given to Venus*, are, on the face of them, folk-tales. Need I give any stronger recommendation of this book to English readers than to ask them to regard it as a sort of outhouse to that goodly fabric so appropriately known to us all as *The Earthly Paradise?*

JOSEPH JACOBS.

CONTENTS

THE TALE OF KING COUSTANS
THE EMPEROR

THE FRIENDSHIP OF AMIS AND AMILE

THE TALE OF KING FLORUS AND
THE FAIR JEHANE

THE HISTORY OF OVER SEA

Of the daughter of the Count of Ponthieu—The
Count taketh Messire Thibault to him—Thibault tells the Count of his love—The Lady
willeth the wedding—Thibault would go a
pilgrimage—He granteth it—She craves to go
with him—The Count comes to know of it—
They go their ways—Messire Thibault and the
lady tarry—They two enter the forest alone—
They go astray—They fall in with strong
thieves—Messire Thibault makes a good defence
—He is overthrown and bound—What they do
with the Lady—Messire Thibault would have
her unloose him—A strange stroke—They come
to their company—They go on their way—
Messire Thibault does his pilgrimage—He comes
back to his own land—The Count asks Thibault
for a tale—He telleth of that adventure as a
tale—The Count is wroth—He would have the
name of the knight—Messire Thibault telleth
him thereof—The Count asketh his daughter
thereof—The Count taketh his daughter on the
sea—The Count's cruel justice—Of the grief of
those others—Of a merchant ship—They get
the tun aboard—They find the lady therein—
She prayeth them mercy—They come to Aumarie—Of the Soudan of Aumarie—He loveth

THE TALE OF KING COUS-TANS THE EMPEROR

THIS tale telleth us that there was *The Tale* erewhile an Emperor of Byzance, *of King* which as now is called Constantinople ; *Coustans* but anciently it was called Byzance. There *the Em-* was in the said city an Emperor ; pagan he *peror* was, and was held for wise as of his law. He knew well enough of a science that is called Astronomy, and he knew withal of the course of the stars, and the planets, and the moon : and he saw well in the stars many marvels, and he knew much of other things wherein the paynims much study, and in the lots they trow, and the answers of the Evil One, that is to say, the Enemy. This Emperor had to name Musselin ; he knew much of lore and of sorceries, as many a pagan doth even yet.

NOW it befell on a time that the Emperor Musselin went his ways a nighttide, he and a knight of his alone together, amidst of the city which is now called Constantinople, and the moon shone full clear.

3

AND so far they went, till they heard a Christian woman who travailed in child-bed in a certain house whereby they went. There was the husband of the said woman aloft in a high solar, and was praying to God one while that she might be delivered, and then again another while that she might not be delivered.

WHEN the Emperor had hearkened this a great while, he said to the knight : "Hast thou heard it of yonder churl how he prayeth that his wife may be delivered of her child, and another while prayeth that she may not be delivered? Certes, he is worser than a thief. For every man ought to have pity of women, more especially of them that be sick of childing. And now, so help me Mahoume and Termagaunt ! if I do not hang him, if he betake him not to telling me reason wherefore he doeth it ! Come we now unto him."

THEY went within, and said the Emperor : "Now churl, tell me of a sooth wherefore thou prayedst thy God thus for thy wife, one while that she might be delivered, and another while that she might be delivered not. This have I will to wot."

4

"SIR," said he, "I will tell thee well. Sooth it is that I be a clerk, and know mickle of a science which men call Astronomy. Withal I wot of the course of the stars and of the planets; therefore saw I well that if my wife were delivered at the point and the hour whereas I prayed God that she might not be delivered, that if she were delivered at that hour, the child would go the way of perdition, and that needs must he be burned, or hanged, or drowned. But whenas I saw that it was good hour and good point, then prayed I to God that she might be delivered. And so sore have I prayed God, that he hath hearkened my prayer of his mercy, and that she is delivered in good point. God be heried and thanked!"

"TELL me now," said the Emperor, "in what good point is the child born?" "Sir," said he, "of a good will; know sir, for sooth, that this child, which here is born, shall have to wife the daughter of the emperor of this city, who was born but scarce eight days ago; and he shall be emperor withal, and lord of this city, and of all the earth." "Churl," said the Emperor, "this which thou sayest can never come to pass." "Sir," said he, "it is all sooth, and thus it behoveth it to be." "Certes," quoth the Emperor, "'tis a mighty matter to trow in."

BUT the Emperor and the Knight departed thence, and the Emperor bade the Knight go bear off the child in such wise, if he might, that none should see him therein. The Knight went and found there two women, who were all busied in arraying the woman who had been brought to bed. The child was wrapped in linen clothes, and they had laid him on a chair. Thereto came the Knight, and took the child and laid him on a board, and brought him to the Emperor, in such wise that none of the women wotted thereof. The Emperor did do slit the belly of him with a knife from the breast down to the navel, and said withal to the Knight, that never should the son of that churl have to wife his daughter, nor be emperor after him.

THEREWITHAL would the Emperor do the Knight to put forth his hand to the belly, to seek out the heart ; but the Knight said to him: "Ah, sir, a-God's mercy, what wouldst thou do ? It is nought meet to

6

thee, and if folk were to wot thereof, great reproach wouldst thou get thee. Let him be at this present, for he is more than dead. And if it please thee that that one trouble more about the matter, I will bear him down to the sea to drown him." "Yea," quoth the Emperor, "bear him away thither, for right sore do I hate him."

SO the Knight took the child, and wrapped him in a cover-point of silk, and bore him down toward the sea. But therewith had he pity of the child, and said that by him should he never be drowned ; so he left him, all wrapped up as he was, on a midden before the gate of a certain abbey of monks, who at that very nick of time were singing their matins.

WHEN the monks had done singing their matins, they heard the child crying, and they bore him before the Lord Abbot. And the Abbot saw that the child was fair, and said that he would do it to be nourished. Therewith he did do unwrap it, and saw that it had the belly cloven from the breast down to the navel.

THE Abbot, so soon as it was day, bade come leeches, and asked of them for how much they would heal the child ;

and they craved for the healing of him an hundred of bezants. But he said that it would be more than enough, for overmuch would the child be costing. And so much did the Abbot, that he made market with the surgeons for four-score bezants. And thereafter the Abbot did do baptize the child, and gave him to name Coustans, because him-seemed that he costed exceeding much for the healing of him.

THE leeches went so much about with the child, that he was made whole : and the Abbot sought him a good nurse, and got the child to suckle, and he was healed full soon ; whereas the flesh of him was soft and tender, and grew together swiftly one to the other, but ever after showed the mark.

MUCH speedily waxed the child in great beauty ; when he was seven years old the Abbot did him to go to the school, and he learned so well, that he over-passed all his fellows in subtilty and science. When he was of twelve years, he was a child exceeding goodly ; so it might nought avail to seek a goodlier. And whenas the Abbot saw him to be a child so goodly and gentle, he did him to ride abroad with him.

8

NOW so it fell out, that the Abbot had to speak with the Emperor of a wrong which his bailiffs had done to the abbey. The Abbot made him a goodly gift, whereas the abbey and convent were subject unto him, for the Emperor was a Saracen. When the Abbot had given him his goodly gift, the Emperor gave him day for the third day thence, whenas he should be at a castle of his, three leagues from the city of Byzance.

THE Abbot abode the day : when he saw the time at point to go to the Emperor, he mounted a-horseback, and his chaplain, and esquire, and his folk ; and with him was Coustans, who was so well fashioned that all praised his great beauty, and each one said that he seemed well to be come of high kindred, and that he would come to great good.

SO when the Abbot was come before the castle whereas the Emperor should be, he came before him and spake to and greeted him : and the Emperor said to him that he should come into the castle, and he would speak with him of his matter : the Abbot made him obeisance, and said to him : "Sir, a-God's name !" Then the

9

Abbot called to him Coustans, who was holding of his hat while he spake unto the Emperor ; and the Emperor looked on the lad, and saw him so fair and gentle as never before had he seen the like fair person. So he asked of the Abbot what he was ; and the Abbot said him that he wotted not, save that he was of his folk, and that he had bred him up from a little child. "And if I had leisure with thee, I would tell thee thereof fine marvels." "Yea," said the Emperor; "come ye into the castle, and therein shalt thou say me the sooth."

THE Emperor came into the castle, and the Abbot was ever beside him, as one who had his business to do ; and he did it to the best that he might, as he who was subject unto him. The Emperor forgat in nowise the great beauty of the lad, and said unto the Abbot that he should cause him come before him, and the Abbot sent for the lad, who came straightway.

WHEN the child was before the Emperor, he seemed unto him right fair ; and he said unto the Abbot, that great damage it was that so fair a lad was Christian. But the Abbot said that it was

10

great joy thereof, whereas he would render unto God a fair soul. When the Emperor heard that, he fell a-laughing, and said to the Abbot that the Christian law was of no account, and that all they were lost who trowed therein. When the Abbot heard him so say, he was sore grieved ; but he durst not make answer as he would, so he said much humbly : "Sir, if God please, who can all things, they are not lost ; for God will have mercy of his sinners."

THEN the Emperor asked of him whence that fair child was come ; and the Abbot said that it was fifteen years gone since he had been found before their gate, on a midden, all of a night-tide. "And our monks heard him a-crying whenas they had but just said matins ; and they went to seek the child, and brought him to me ; and I looked on the babe, and beheld him much fair, and I said that I would do him to be nourished and bap- tized. I unwrapped him, for the babe was wrapped up in a cover-point of vermil sendel ; and when he was unwrapped, I saw that he had the belly slit from the breast to the navel. Then I sent for leeches and surgeons, and made market with them to heal him for four-score bezants ; and thereafter he was baptized, and I gave him to name Coustans, because he costed so much of goods to heal. So was the babe presently made whole : but never sithence might it be that the mark appeared not on his belly."

WHEN the Emperor heard that, he knew that it was the child whose belly he had slit to draw the heart out of him. So he said to the Abbot that he should give him the lad. And the Abbot said that he would speak thereof to his convent, and that he should have him with their good-will. The Emperor held his peace, and answered never a word. But the Abbot took leave of him, and came to his abbey, and his monks, and told them that the Emperor had craved Coustans of him. " But I answered that I would speak to you if ye will yea-say it. Say, now, what ye would praise of my doing herein."

" WHAT ! " said the wisest of the convent; " by our faith, evil hast thou done, whereas thou gavest him not presently, even as he demanded of thee. We counsel thee send him straightway, lest the

12

Emperor be wrath against us, for speedily may we have scathe of him."

THERETO was their counsel fast, that Coustans should be sent to the Em- peror. So the Abbot commanded the Prior to lead Coustans thereto ; and the Prior said : " A–God's name ! "

SO he mounted, and led with him Coustans, and came unto the Emperor, and greeted him on behalf of the Abbot and the convent ; and then he took Coustans by the hand, and, on the said behalf, gave him to the Emperor, who received him as one who was much wrath that such a runagate and beggar churl should have his daughter to wife. But he thought in 'his heart that he would play him the turn.

WHEN the Emperor had gotten Coustans, he was in sore imagination how he should be slain in such wise that none might wot word thereof. And it fell out so that the Emperor had matters on hand at the outer marches of his land, much long aloof thence, well a twelve days' journey. So the Emperor betook him to going thither, and had Coustans thither with him, and thought what wise he might to do slay him, till at last he let write a letter to his Burgreve of Byzance.

" I EMPEROR of Byzance and Lord of Greece, do thee to wit who abidest duly in my place for the warding of my land ; and so soon as thou seest this letter thou shalt slay or let slay him who this letter shall bear to thee, so soon as he hast delivered the said letter to thee, without longer tarrying. As thou holdest dear thine own proper body, do straightway my commandment herein."

E VEN such was the letter which the fair child Coustans bore, and knew not that he bore his own death. The lad took the letter, which was close, and betook him to the road, and did so much by his journeys that he came in less than fifteen days to Byzance, which is nowadays called Constantinople.

W HEN the lad entered into the city, it was the hour of dinner ; so, as God would have it, he thought that he would not go his errand at that nick of time, but would tarry till folk had done dinner : and exceeding hot was the weather, as is wont about St. John's-mass. So he entered into the garden all a-horseback. Great and long

14

was the garden ; so the lad took the bridle
from off his horse and unlaced the saddle-
girths, and let him graze ; and thereafter
he went into the nook of a tree ; and full
pleasant was the place, so that presently he
fell asleep.

NOW so it fell out, that when the fair daughter of the Emperor had eaten, she went into the garden with three of her maidens ; and they fell to chasing each other about, as whiles is the wont of maidens to play ; until at the last the fair Emperor's daughter came under the tree whereas Coustans lay a-sleeping, and he was all vermil as the rose. And when the damsel saw him, she beheld him with a right good will, and she said to herself that never on a day had she seen so fair a fashion of man. Then she called to her that one of her fellows in whom she had the most affiance, and the others she made to go forth from out of the garden.

THEN the fair maiden, daughter of the Emperor, took her fellow by the hand, and led her to look on the lovely lad whereas he lay a-sleeping ; and she spake thus : " Fair fellow, here is a rich treasure. Lo thou ! the most fairest fashion of a

15

man that ever mine eyes have seen on any day of my life. And he beareth a letter, and well I would see what it sayeth."

SO the two maidens drew nigh to the lad, and took from him the letter, and the daughter of the Emperor read the same; and when she had read it, she fell a-lamenting full sore, and said to her fellow: "Certes here is a great grief!" "Ha, my Lady!" said the other one, "tell me what it is." "Of a surety," said the Maiden, "might I but trow in thee I would do away that sorrow!" "Ha, Lady," said she, "hardily mayest thou trow in me, whereas for nought would I uncover that thing which thou wouldst have hid."

THEN the Maiden, the daughter of the Emperor, took oath of her according to the paynim law; and thereafter she told her what the letter said; and the damsel answered her: "Lady, and what wouldest thou do?" "I will tell thee well," said the daughter of the Emperor; "I will put in his pouch another letter, wherein the Emperor, my father, biddeth his Burgreve to give me to wife to this fair child here, and that he make great feast at the doing of the wedding unto all the folk of this land; whereas

16

he is to wot well that the lad is a high man *The Tale*
and a loyal." *of King*
WHEN the damsel had heard that, she *Coustans*
said that would be good to do. "But, *the Em-*
Lady, how wilt thou have the seal of thy *peror*
father?" "Full well," said the Maiden, "for
my father delivered to me four pair of scrolls,
sealed of his seal thereon ; he hath written
nought therein ; and I will write all that I
will." "Lady," said she, "thou hast said full
well ; but do it speedily, and haste thee
ere he awakeneth." "So will I," said the
Maiden.

THEN the fair Maiden, the daughter of
the Emperor, went to her coffers, and
drew thereout one of the said scrolls sealed,
which her father had left her, that she
might borrow moneys thereby, if so she
would. For ever was the Emperor and his
folk in war, whereas he had neighbours
right felon, and exceeding mighty, whose
land marched upon his. So the Maiden
wrote the letter in this wise :

"I KING MUSSELIN, Emperor of Greece
and of Byzance the city, to my Burgreve
of Byzance greeting. I command thee that
the bearer of this letter ye give to my fair
daughter in marriage according to our law;

whereas I have heard and wot soothly that he is a high person, and well worthy to have my daughter. And thereto make ye great joy and great feast to all them of my city and of all my land."

IN such wise wrote and said the letter of the fair daughter of the Emperor ; and when she had written the said letter, she went back to the garden, she and her fellow together, and found that one yet asleep, and they put the letter into his pouch. And then they began to sing and make noise to awaken him. So he awoke anon, and was all astonied at the fair Maiden, the daughter of the Emperor, and the other one her fellow, who came before him ; and the fair Maiden, daughter of the Emperor, greeted him ; and he greeted her again right debonairly. Then she asked of him what he was, and whither he went ; and he said that he bore a letter to the Burgreve, which the Emperor sent by him ; and the Maiden said that she would bring him straightway whereas was the Burgreve. Therewith she took him by the hand, and brought him to the palace, where there was much folk, who all rose against the Maiden, as to her who was their Lady.

18

NOW the Maiden demanded the Bur- *The Tale*greve, and they told her that he was *of King* in a chamber; so thither she led the lad, *Coustans* and the lad delivered the letter, and said *the Em-* that the Emperor greeted him. But the *peror* Burgreve made great joy of the lad, and kissed the hand of him. The Maiden opened the pouch, and fell a-kissing the letter and the seal of her father for joy's sake, whereas she had not heard tidings of him a great while.

THEREAFTER she said to the Burgreve that she would hearken the letter in privy council, even as if she wotted nought thereof; and the Burgreve said that that were good to do. Then went the Burgreve and the Maiden into a chamber, and the Maiden unfolded the letter and read it to the Burgreve, and made semblance of wondering exceedingly; and the Burgreve said to her, "Lady, it behoveth to do the will of my lord thy father, for otherwise we shall be blamed exceedingly." The Maiden answered him: "And how can this be, that I should be wedded without my lord my father? A strange thing it would be, and I will do it in no manner."

19

"HA, Lady!" said the Burgreve, "what is that thou sayest? Thy father has bidden thus by his letter, and it behoveth not to gainsay."

"SIR," said the Maiden, (unto whom it was late till the thing were done) "thou shalt speak unto the barons and mighty men of this realm, and take counsel thereof. And if they be of accord thereto, I am she who will not go against it." Then the Burgreve said that she spake well and as one wise.

THEN spake the Burgreve to the barons, and showed them the letter, and they accorded all to that that the matter of the letter must be accomplished, and the will of the Emperor done. Then they wedded the fair youth Coustans, according to the paynim law, unto the fair daughter of the Emperor; and the wedding endured for fifteen days : and such great joy was there at Byzance that it was exceeding, and folk did no work in the city, save eating and drinking and making merry.

LONG while abode the Emperor in the land whereas he was: and when he had done his business, he went his ways back towards Byzance; and whenas he was but

20

anigh two journeys thence, came to him a message of the messengers who came from Byzance. The Emperor asked of him what they did in the city; and the varlet said that they were making exceeding good cheer of eating and drinking and taking their ease, and that no work had they done therein these fifteen days.

"AND wherefore is that?" said the Emperor. "Wherefore, Sir! Wot ye not well thereof?" "Nay, forsooth," said the Emperor, "but tell me wherefore."

"SIR," said the varlet, "thou sentest a youngling, exceeding fair, to thy Burgreve, and badest him by thy letter to wed him to thy daughter the fair, and that he should be emperor after thee, whereas he was a man right high, and well worthy to have her. But thy daughter would not take that before that the Burgreve should have spoken to the barons. And he spake to all them, and showed them thy letter; and they said that it behoved to do thy commandment. And when thy daughter saw that they were all of one accord thereon, she durst not go against them, but yeasaid it. Even in such wise hath thy daughter been wedded, and such joy has

21

been in the city as none might wish it better."

THE Emperor, when he heard the messenger speak thus, was all astonied, and thought much of this matter ; and he asked of the varlet how long it was since the lad had wedded his daughter, and whether or no he had lain by her?

"SIR," said the varlet, "yea ; and she may well be big by now; because it is more than three weeks since he hath wedded her." "Forsooth," said the Emperor, "in a good hour be it! for since it is so, it behoveth me to abide it, since no other it may be."

SO far rode the Emperor till he came to Byzance, whereas they made him much fair feast ; and his fair daughter came to meet him, and her husband Coustans, who was so fair a child that none might better be. The Emperor, who was a wise man, made of them much great joy, and laid his two hands upon their two heads, and held them there a great while ; which is the manner of benison amongst the paynims.

THAT night thought the Emperor much on this marvel, how it could have come about ; and so much he pondered it, that he wotted full well that it had been

because of his daughter. So he had no *The Tale*
will to gain-say her, but he demanded to *of King*
see the letter which he had sent, and they *Coustans*
showed it unto him, and he saw his seal *the Em-*
hanging thereto, and saw the letter which *peror*
was written ; and by the manner whereby the
thing had been done, he said to himself
that he had striven against the things which
behoved to be.

THEREAFTER, the Emperor made
Coustans a knight, even his new son
who was wedded unto his daughter, and he
gave and granted to him all the whole land
after his death. And the said Coustans
bore him well and wisely, as a good knight,
and a valiant and hardy, and defended him
full well against his enemies. No long
time wore ere his lord the Emperor died,
and his service was done much richly, after
the paynim law. Then was Coustans emperor, and he loved and honoured much the
Abbot who had nourished him, and he made
him his very master. And the Emperor
Coustans, by the counsel of the Abbot, and
the will of God the all mighty, did do
christen his wife, and all they of that land
were converted to the law of Jesus Christ.
And the Emperor Coustans begot on his

23

wife an heir male, who had to name Constantine, who was thereafter a prudhomme much great. And thereafter was the city called Constantinople, because of his father, Coustans, who costed so much, but aforetime was it called Byzance.

HERE withal endeth the Story of King Coustans the Emperor.

The said story was done out of the ancient French into English by William Morris.

THE FRIENDSHIP OF
AMIS AND AMILE

I N the time of Pepin King of France was *The* a child born in the Castle of Bericain of *Friend-* a noble father of Alemaine who was of great *ship of* holiness. *Amis and*

The father and the mother promised to *Amile* God, and Saint Peter and Saint Paul, whereas they had none other child, that if God gave it life, they would bear it to Rome to · baptism. At the same time came a vision to a Count of Alverne, whose wife was big with child, whereby it seemed that the Apostle of Rome was baptizing many children in his palace and confirming them with chrism.

So when the Count was awaken he sought of many wise folk what might signify that which he had seen in the dream. And when his vision was uncovered, a wise man and ancient bespake him by the counsel of God : " Make great joy, Count, for there shall be born to thee a son full of great prowess and of great holiness ; and him thou

shalt let bear to Rome and let baptize him
by the Apostle."

Thereof great joy made the Count, and
he and his folk praised the counsel of the
elder.

THE child was born and dearly fostered,
and when he had two years, and the
father after his purpose was bearing him to
Rome, he came to the city of Lucca. And
therein he found a noble man of Almaine
who was wending Romeward and bearing
his son to baptism. They greeted one the
other, and each asked other who he was and
what he sought, and when they found themselves to be of one purpose they joined
company in all friendliness and entered
Rome together. And the two children fell
to loving one another so sorely that one
would not eat without the other, they lived
of one victual, and lay in one bed.

IN this wise the fathers brought them
before the Apostle at Rome, and spake
to him : "Holy Father, whom we know
and believe to be in the place of Saint Peter
the Apostle, the Count of Alverne, and a
noble knight of Bericain the Castle, beseech
your Holiness that ye would deign to baptize their sons which they have brought from

far away, and that ye would take their little
offering from their hands."

AND the Apostle answered them : " I
hold your gifts for right acceptable,
but they are not to me of much necessity ;
give them to the poor, who have need
thereof. The infants will I baptize with a
good will, that the Father, the Son, and the
Holy Ghost may embrace them in the love
of the Holy Trinity."

FORTHWITH then the Apostle baptized them in the Church of the Holy
Saviour, and laid for name on the son of
the Count, Amile, and on the son of the
Knight, Amis ; and many a knight of Rome
held them at the font with mickle joy, and
raised them aloft even as God would. And
the office of Baptism done, the Apostle bade
bring two hanaps of tree dight with gold
and precious stones, side and wide alike, and
of like fashion, and gave them to the bairns
and said : " Take these gifts in token that
I have baptized you in the Church of the
Holy Saviour." Which gifts they took
joyfully and thanked him much, and betook them thence home in all joyance.

TO the child of Bericain did God give
so great wisdom, that one might trow

29

that he were another Solomon ; and when
he was of the age of thirty years a fever
took his father, and he fell to admonishing
his son in such like words : "Fair son, well
beloved, it behoveth me presently to die,
and thou shalt abide and be thine own
master. Now firstly, fair son, keep thou
the commandments of God ; the chivalry
of Jesus Christ do thou. Keep thou faith
to thy lords, and give aid to thy fellows
and friends. Defend the widows and
orphans. Uphold the poor and needy :
and all days hold thy last day in memory.
Forget not the fellowship and friendship of
the son of the Count of Alverne, whereas the
Apostle of Rome on one day baptized you
both, and with one gift honoured you. Ye
be alike of beauty, of fashion, and stature,
and whoso should see you, would deem you
to be brethren."

SO having finished these words, and received his Saviour, he departed in our
Lord, and his son did do bury him, and did
do render him his service, even as one
should do for the dead.

AFTER the death of his father evil folk
bore envy against him, and did him
many a scathe, and grieved him sorely ;
30

but he loved them all and suffered whatso- *The*
ever they did to him.   What more may I *Friend-*
tell you, save that they cast him and his *ship of*
folk out of the heritage of his fathers, and *Amis and*
chased him forth out of his castle.   So when *Amile*
he bethought him of the commandment of
his father, he said to them who went in his
company : " The wicked have wrongfully
cast me forth out of mine heritage : yet
have I good hope in our Lord that he will
help me ; go we now to the Court of
the Count Amile, who was my friend and
my fellow.   May-happen he will make us
rich with his goods and his havings.   But
if it be not so, then shall we go to Hilde-
gard the Queen, wife of King Charles of
France, who is wont to comfort the disinherited."

AND they answered that they were ready
to follow him and do his bidding.

THEREWITH they went their ways
to the Court of the Count and found
him not there, because he was gone to
Bericain to visit Amis his fellow, and comfort
him of the death of his father.   And when
he found him not, he departed sore troubled,
and said to himself that he would not betake him to his own land till he had found

31

Amis his fellow ; and he sought him in France and in Almaine, where soever he heard tell that his kindred were, and could find no certainty of him.

THEREWITHAL Amis together with his folk, ceased not to seek his fellow Amile, until they came to the house of a noble man where they were guested. Thereat they told by order all their adventure ; and the noble man said to them : "Abide with me, Sir Knights, and I will give my daughter to your lord, because of the wisdom that I have heard of him, and I will make you all rich of gold and of silver, and of havings."

THAT word pleased them, and they held the bridal with mickle joy. But when they had abided there for a year and a half, then said Amis to his ten fellows : "We have done amiss in that we have left seeking of Amile." And he left there two of his sergeants and his hanap, and went his ways toward Paris.

NOW by this time had Amile been a-seeking for Amis two years past without ceasing. And whenas Amile drew nigh to Paris he found a pilgrim and asked if he had seen Amis whom men had chased out of his land ; and that one said nay, he had not. But Amile did off his coat and gave it to the pilgrim and said : "Pray thou to our Lord and his Hallows that they give me to find Amis my fellow."

THEN he departed from the pilgrim, and went his ways to Paris, and found no-whither Amis his fellow.

BUT the pilgrim went his ways forthwith, and about vespers happened on Amis, and they greeted each the other. And Amis said to the pilgrim, had he seen or heard tidings in any land of Amile, son of the Count of Alverne. And the pilgrim answered him all marvelling : "Who art thou, Knight, who thus mockest a pilgrim ? Thou seemest to me that Amile who this day asked of me if I had seen Amis his fellow. I wot not for why thou hast changed thy garments, thy folk, thine horses, and thine arms. Thou askest me now what thou didst ask me to-day about tierce ; and thou gavest me this coat."

TROUBLE not thine heart," said Amis, "I am not he whom thou deemest ; but I am Amis who seeketh Amile." And he gave him of his silver, and bade him pray our Lord to give him to find Amile. And the pilgrim said : "Go thy ways forthright to Paris, and I trow that thou shalt find him whom thou seekest so sore longing." And therewith Aims went his ways full eagerly.

NOW on the morrow Amile was already departed from Paris, and was sitting at meat with his knights hard by the water of Seine in a flowery meadow. And when they saw Amis coming with his fellows all armed, they rose up and armed them, and so went forth before them ; and Amis said to his fellows : " I see French knights who come against us in arms. Now fight hardily and defend your lives. If we may escape this peril, then shall we go with great joy to Paris, and thereto shall we be received with high favour at the Court of the King."

Then were the reins let loose and the spears shaken aloft, and the swords drawn on either side, in such wise that no sem-blance was there that any should escape alive. But God the all mighty who seeth all, and who setteth an end to the toil of the righteous, did to hold aback them of one part and of the other when they were now hard on each other, for then said Amis : " Who are ye knights, who have

34

will to slay Amis the exile and his fellows ?"
At that voice Amile knew Amis his fellow
and said : "O thou Amis most well beloved, rest from my travail, I am Amile,
son of the Count of Alverne, who have not
ceased to seek thee for two whole years."

AND therewith they lighted down from their horses, and embraced and kissed each other, and gave thanks to God of that they were found. And they swore fealty and friendship and fellowship perpetual, the one to the other, on the sword of Amile, wherein were relics. Thence went they all together to the Court of Charles, King of France ; there might men behold them young, well attempered, wise, fair, and of like fashion and visage, loved of all and honoured. And the King received them much joyously, and made of Amis his treasurer, and of Amile his server.

BUT when they had abided thus three years, Amis said unto Amile : "Fair sweet fellow, I desire sore to go see my wife whom I have left behind ; and I will return the soonest that I may ; and do thou abide at the Court. But keep thee well from touching the daughter of the King ; and above all things beware of

Arderi the felon." Amile answered him : "I will take heed of thy commandment ; but betake thee back hither so soon as thou mayest."

THUSWISE departed Amis. But Amile cast his eyes upon the King's daughter, and knew her so soon as he might ; and right soon forgat he the commandment and the teaching of Amis his fellow. Yet is not this adventure strange, whereas he was no holier than David, nor wiser than Solomon.

AMIDST these things Arderi the traitor, who bore him envy, came to him and said : "Thou wottest not, fellow, thou wottest not, how Amis hath robbed the treasure of the King, and therefore is fled away. Wherefore I require of thee thou swear me fealty and friendship and fellowship, and I will swear the same to thee on the holy Gospel." And so when that was done Amile doubted not to lay bare his secret to Arderi.

BUT whenas Amile was a-giving water to the King to wash his hands withal, the false Arderi said to the King : "Take thou no water from this evil man, sir King : for he is more worthy of death than

36

of life, whereas he hath taken from the Queen's Daughter the flower of her virginity." But when Amile heard this, he fell adown all astonied, and might say never a word ; but the benign King lifted him up again, and said to him : " Rise up, Amile, and have no fear, and defend thee of this blame." So he lifted himself up and said : " Have no will to trow, sire, in the lies of Arderi the traitor, for I wot that thou art a rightwise judge, and that thou turnest not from the right way, neither for love nor for hatred. Wherefore I pray thee that thou give me frist of counsel ; and that I may purge me of this guilt before thee, and do the battle against Arderi the traitor, and make him convict of his lies before all the Court."

SO the King gave to one and the other frist of counsel till after nones, and that then they should come before him for to do their devoir ; and they came before the King at the term which he had given them. Arderi brought with him the Count Herbert for his part ; but Amile found none who would be for him saving Hildegarde the Queen, who took up the cause for him, and gat frist of counsel for

Amile, on such covenant that if Amile
came not back by the term established, she
should be lacking all days of the bed of the
King.

BUT when Amile went to seek counsel,
he happened on Amis, his fellow, who
was betaking him to the King's Court ;
and Amile lighted down from his horse,
and cast himself at the feet of his fellow,
and said : " O thou, the only hope of my
salvation, evilly have I kept thy commandment ; for I have run into wyte of the
King's Daughter, and I have taken up
battle against the false Arderi."

THEN said Amis, sighing : " Leave we
here our folk, end enter into this wood
to lay bare our secret." And Amis fell to
blaming Amile, and said : " Change we
our garments and our horses, and get thee
to my house, and I will do the battle for
thee against the traitor." And Amile answered : "How may I go into thine house,
who have no knowledge of thy wife and
thy folk, and have never seen them face to
face ?" But Amis said to him : " Go in
all safety, and seek wisely to know them :
but take good heed that thou touch not my
wife."

38

AND thuswise they departed each from his fellow weeping ; and Amis went his ways to the Court of the King in the semblance of Amile, and Amile to the house of his fellow in the semblance of Amis. But the wife of Amis, when she saw him betake him thither, ran to embrace him, whom she deemed was her husband, and would have kissed him. But he said : "Flee thou from before me, for I have greater need to lament than to play ; whereas, since I departed from thee, I have suffered adversity full sore, and yet have to suffer."

AND a night-time whenas they lay in one bed, then Amile laid his sword betwixt the two of them, and said to the woman : "Take heed that thou touch me in no manner wise, else diest thou straightway by this sword." And in like-wise did he the other nights, until Amis betook him in disguise to his house to wot if Amile kept faith with him of his wife.

NOW was the term of the battle come, and the Queen abode Amile all full of fear, for the traitor Arderi said, all openly, that the Queen should nevermore draw nigh the bed of the King, whereas she had suffered and consented hereto, that Amile should shame her daughter. Amidst these words Amis entered into the Court of the King clad in the raiment of his fellow, Amile, at the hour of midday and said to the King : " Right debonaire and loyal judge, here am I apparelled to do the battle against the false Arderi, in defence of me, the Queen, and her daughter of the wyte which they lay upon us."

And the King answered benignly and said : "Be thou nought troubled, Count, for if thou vanquishest the battle, I will give thee to wife Belisant my daughter."

ON the morrow's morn, Arderi and Amis entered armed into the field in the presence of the King and his folk. And the Queen with much company of virgins, and widows and wedded wives, went from church to church making prayers for the Champion of her daughter, and they gave gifts, oblations and candles.

BUT Amis fell to pondering in his heart, that if he should slay Arderi, he would be guilty of his death before God, and if he were vanquished, it should be for a reproach to him all his days.

40

Wherefore he spake thuswise to Arderi : *The*
" O thou, Count, foul rede thou hast, in *Friend-*
that thou desirest my death so sorely, and *ship of*
hast foolishly cast thy life into peril of *Amis and*
death. If thou wouldest but take back *Amile*
the wyte which thou layest on me, and
leave this mortal battle, thou mayest have
my friendship and my service."

BUT Arderi, as one out of his wit,
answered him : " I will nought of thy
friendship nor thy service ; but I shall
swear the sooth as it verily is, and I shall
smite the head from off thee."

SO Arderi swore that he had shamed the
King's Daughter, and Amis swore that
he lied ; and straightway they dealt together in strokes, and fought together from
the hour of tierce right on till nones. And
Arderi was vanquished, and Amis smote off
his head.

THE King was troubled that he had
lost Arderi ; yet was he joyous that
his daughter was purged of her guilt. And
he gave to Amis his daughter, and a great
sum of gold and silver, and a city hard by
the sea wherein to dwell. And Amis received the same with great joy. Then he
returned at his speediest to his hostel

wherein he had left Amile his fellow ; but whenas Amile saw him coming with much company of horse, he deemed that Amis was vanquished, and fell to fleeing : but Amis bade him return in all safety, for that he had vanquished Arderi, and thereby was wedded for him to the King's Daughter. Thence then did Amile betake him, and abode in the aforesaid city with his wife.

BUT Amis abode with his wife, and he became mesel by the will of our Lord, in such wise that he might not move from his bed ; for God chastiseth him that He loveth.

AND his wife, who had to name Obias, had him in sore hate, and many a time strove to strangle him ; and when Amis found that, he called to him two of his sergeants, Azones and Horatus by name, and said to them : " Take me out of the hands of this evil woman, and take my hanap privily and bear me to the Castle of Beri-cain."

SO when they drew nigh to the castle, folk came to meet them, and asked of them who was the feeble sick man whom they bore ; and they said it was Amis, the master of them, who was become mesel, and

42

prayed them that they would do him some
mercy. But nevertheless, they beat the
sergeants of Amis, and cast him down from
the cart whereon they were bearing him,
and said : "Flee hence speedily if ye would
not lose your lives."

THEN Amis fell a-weeping, and said :
"O Thou, God debonaire and full of
pity, give me death, or give me aid from
mine infirmity !" And therewith he said
to his sergeants : "Bring me to the Church
of the Father of Rome, whereas God may
peradventure of His great mercy purvey for
my poverty."

WHEN they came to Rome, Constantin
the Apostle, full of pity and of holiness, and many a knight of Rome of them
who had held Amis at the font, came to
meet him, and gave him sustenance enough
for him and his sergeants.

BUT in the space of three years thereafter was so great famine in the city,
that the father had will to thrust the son
away from his house. Then spake Azones
and Horatus to Amis, and said : "Fair sir,
thou wottest how feally we have served thee
sithence the death of thy father unto this
day, and that we have never trespassed

against thy commandment. But now we may no longer abide with thee, whereas we have no will to perish of hunger: wherefore we pray thee give us leave to escape this mortal pestilence."

THEN Amis answered them weeping: "O ye fair sons, and not sergeants, my only comfort, I pray you for God's sake that ye leave me not here, but bear me to the city of the Count Amile my fellow."

AND they who would well obey his commandments, bore him thither whereas was Amile; and there they fell to sounding on their tartavelles before the Court of Amile, even as mesel folk be wont to do. And when Amile heard the sound thereof, he bade a sergeant of his to bear to the sick man of bread and of flesh, and therewithal his hanap, which was given to him at Rome, full of good wine: and when the sergeant had done his commandment he said to him when he came again: "By the faith which I owe thee, sir, if I held not thine hanap in my hand, I had deemed that it was even that which the sick man had; for one and the same be they of greatness and of fashion." Then said Amile:

44

"Go speedily and lead him hither to
me."

BUT when he was before his fellow he
asked of him who he was, and how he
had gotten that hanap. Said he: "I am
of Bericain the Castle, and the hanap was
given me by the Apostle of Rome, when he
baptized me."

AND when Amile heard that, he knew
that it was Amis his fellow who had
delivered him from death, and given him to
wife the King's Daughter of France;
straightway he cast himself upon him and
fell to crying out strongly, and to weeping
and lamenting, and to kissing and embracing him. And when his wife heard the
same, she ran thereto all dishevelled, and
making great dole, whereas she had in
memory of how he had slain Arderi. And
straightway they laid him in a very fair bed,
and said to him: "Abide with us, fair sir,
until that God shall do his will of thee, for
whatsoever we have is for thee to deal with."
And he abode with them, and his sergeants
with him.

NOW it befel on a night whenas Amis
and Amile lay in one chamber without
other company, that God sent to Amis

Raphael his angel, who said to him:
"Sleepest thou, Amis?" And he, who
deemed that Amile had called to him,
answered: "I sleep not, fair sweet fellow."
Then the angel said to him: "Thou
hast answered well, whereas thou art the
fellow of the citizens of Heaven, and thou
hast followed after Job, and Thoby in
patience. Now I am Raphael, an angel of
our Lord, and am come to tell thee of a
medicine for thine healing, whereas He
hath heard thy prayers. Thou shalt tell to
Amile thy fellow, that he slay his two
children and wash thee in their blood, and
thence thou shalt get thee the healing of thy
body."

THEN said Amis: "Never shall it be
that my fellow be a manslayer for the
healing of me." But the Angel said: "Yet
even so it behoveth to do."

AND when he had so said, the Angel
departed; and therewith Amile, as if
a-sleeping, heard those words, and awoke,
and said: "What is it, fellow? who hath
spoken unto thee?" And Amis answered
that none had spoken: "But I have prayed
to our Lord according to my wont." Then
Amile said: "Nay, it is not so; some one

46

hath spoken to thee." Therewith he arose *The* and went to the door of the chamber, and *Friend-* found it shut, and said: "Tell me, fair *ship of* brother, who hath spoken to thee these *Amis and* words of the night?" *Amile*

THEN Amis fell a-weeping sorely, and said to him that it was Raphael the Angel of our Lord who had said to him: "Amis, our Lord biddeth that thou tell Amile that he slay his two children, and wash thee with the blood of them, and that then thou wilt be whole of thy meselry."

BUT Amile was sore moved with these words, and said to him: "Amis, I have given over to thee man-servant and maid-servant and all my goods, and now thou feignest in fraud that the Angel hath spoken to thee that I slay my two children!" But forthwith Amis fell a-weeping, and said: "I wot that I have spoken to thee things grievous, as one constrained, and now I pray thee that thou cast me not out of thine house." And Amile said that he had promised that he would hold him till the hour of his death: "But I conjure thee by the faith which is betwixt thee and me, and by our fellowship, and by the

47

baptism which we took between me and thee at Rome, that thou tell me if it be man or Angel who hath said this to thee."

THEN Amis answered : "As true as it was an Angel who spake to me this night, so may God deliver me from mine infirmity."

THEN Amile fell to weeping privily, and thinking in his heart : "This man forsooth was apparelled before the King to die for me, and why should I not slay my children for him ; if he hath kept faith with me to the death, why keep I not faith ? Abraham was saved by faith, and by faith have the hallows vanquished kingdoms ; and God saith in the Gospel : 'That which ye would that men should do unto you, do ye even so to them.'"

AND Amile without more tarrying, went to the chamber of his wife, and bade her go hear the service of our Lord ; and the Countess gat her to the church even as she was wont.

THEN the Count took his sword, and went to the bed where lay his children, and found them sleeping, and he threw himself upon them, and fell to weeping

48

bitterly and said : "Who hath heard ever of a father who of his own will hath slain his child? Ah, alas my children ! I shall be no more your father, but your cruel murderer ! And therewith the children awoke because of the tears which fell on them from their father ; and the children, who looked on the face of their father, fell a-laughing. And whereas they were of the age of three years or thereabout, their father said to them : "Your laughter shall be turned into weeping, for now shall your innocent blood be shed."

WHEN he had so said he cut off their heads and then laid them out behind the bed, and laid the heads to the bodies, and covered them over even as they slept. And with their blood which he received, he washed his fellow, and said : "Sire God, Jesus Christ, who commandest men to keep faith upon the earth, and who cleansest the mesel by thy word, deign thou to cleanse my fellow, for the love of whom I have shed the blood of my children."

THEN was Amis cleansed of his meselry, and they gave thanks to our Lord with great joy and said : "Blessed be God, the father of our Lord Jesus Christ, who healeth them that have hope in him."

AND Amile clad his fellow in his own right goodly raiment ; and therewith they went to the church to give thanks there, and the bells by the grace of God rang of themselves. And when the people of the city heard that, they ran all together toward that marvel.

NOW the wife of the Count when she saw them both going together, fell to asking which of the two was her husband and said : "I know well the raiment of these twain, but I wot not which is Amile."

AND the Count said : " I am Amile, and this my fellow is Amis, who is whole." Then the Countess wondered, and said : "I see him all whole ; but much I desire to know whereby he is healed." " Render we thanks to our Lord," said the Count, "nor disquiet us as to how it may be."

NOW was come the hour of tierce, and neither the father nor the mother was yet entered in to their children ; but the father sighed grievously for the death of his babes. Then the Countess asked for her children to make her joy, and the Count said : " Dame let be, let the children sleep !"

50

Therewith he entered all alone to the chil- *The*
dren to weep over them, and he found them *Friend-*
playing in the bed ; but the scars of their *ship of*
wounds showed about the necks of each of *Amis and*
them even as a red fillet. *Amile*

THEN he took them in his arms, and
bore them to their mother, and said :
" Make great joy, dame, whereas thy sons
whom I had slain by the commandment of
the Angel are alive again, and by their
blood is Amis cured and healed."

AND when the Countess heard it she
said : "O thou, Count, why didst thou
not lead me with thee to receive the blood
of my children, and I would have washed
therewith Amis thy fellow and my Lord?"

THEN said the Count : "Dame, let be
these words ; and let us be at the service of our Lord, who hath done such great
wonders in our house."

Which thing they did even unto their
death and held chastity.

And they made great joy through that
same city for ten days.

BUT on the selfsame day that Amis was
made whole, the devils bore off his
wife ; they brake the neck of her, and bore
away her soul.

AFTER these things Amis betook him
to the Castle of Bericain and laid siege
before it ; and abode there before so long,
that they of the castle rendered themselves
to him. He received them benignly, and
pardoned them their evil will ; and from
thenceforth he dwelt with them peaceably ;
and he held with him the elder son of
Amile, and served our Lord with all his
heart.

THEREAFTER Adrian, Apostle of
Rome, sent word to Charles, King of
France, that he come help him against
Desir, the King of the Lombards, who
much tormented the Church ; and Charles
was as then in the town of Theodocion.
Thither came Peter, messenger of the
Apostle, who said to him that the Apostle
prayed him to come defend Holy Church.
Thereupon King Charles sent to the said
Desir messengers to pray him that he give
back to the Holy Father the cities and
other things which he had taken from him,
and that he would give him thereto the
sum of forty thousand sols of gold in gold
and in silver. But he would give way
neither for prayers nor gifts. Thereon the
good King bade come to him all manner
52

folk, Bishops, Abbots, Dukes, Princes, Mar- *The*
quises and other strong knights. And he *Friend-*
sent to Cluses certain of these for to guard *ship of*
the passage of the ways. Amongst the *Amis and*
which was Albins, Bishop of Angier, a *Amile*
man full of great holiness.

THEN the King Charles together with
many warriors, drew nigh to Cluses by
the Mount of Sinense, and sent Bernhart
his uncle, and a many with him, by the
Mount of Jove. And the vanward said
that Desir, together with all his force,
was already at Cluses, the which he had
do dight with bulwarks of iron and
stone.

BUT whenas Charles drew nigh to Cluses,
he sent his messengers to Desir, praying him to give back to the Holy Father
the cities which he had taken ; but he would
nought for the prayer. Again Charles bade
him that he send three of the children of
the judges of Lombardy in hostage, until
such time as he had given back the cities of
the Church, and that he would betake him
to France with all his host, without battle
and without doing any scathe. But he
neither for that, nor for aught else would
blench one whit.

53

NOW when God the almighty had seen the hard heart and malice of this man ; and that the French were sore desirous to get them aback home, he set so great fear and so great trembling in the hearts of the Lombards, that they turned to flight all of them, although none chased them, and left there behind them their tents and all their gear. When that saw Charles and his host, they followed them and thrust forth into Lombardy French, Almaines, English and all other manner of folk.

OF that host were Amis and Amile, who were the first in the court of the King, and every way they heeded the works of our Lord, in fasting, in praying, in alms-doing, in giving aid to widows and orphans, in often times appeasing the wrath of the King, in suffering the evil, and consoling the realm of the Romans.

NOW whenas Charles had much folk in Lombardy, King Desir came to meet him with his little host; for whereas Desir had a priest, Charles had a bishop ; whereas that one had a monk, the other had an abbot ; where Desir had a knight Charles had a prince ; the one had a man afoot,

the other a duke or a count. What should *The*
I say, where that King had one knight, *Friend-*
Charles had thirty. So the two hosts fell *ship of*
to blows together with great cries and ban- *Amis and*
ners displayed ; stones and darts flying here *Amile*
and there, and knights falling on every
part.

AND the Lombards fought so mightily
for three days, that they slew of King
Charles a very great infinity. And after
the third day's wearing Charles called to
him the most mighty and the strongest of
his host, and said to them : " Either die ye
in battle, or gain ye the victory."

SO the King Desir and the whole host of
the Lombards together fled away to the
place hight Mortara, which in those days
was called Fair-wood, whereas thereabout
was the land delectable : there they refreshed them and took heed to their
horses.

ON the morrow morn King Charles and
his host came thither, and found the
Lombards all armed, and there they joined
battle, and a great multitude of dead there
was on one side and the other, and because
of this slaughter had the place to name
Mortara.

MOREOVER, there died Amis and
Amile, for even as God had joined
them together by good accord in their life-
days, so in their death they were not sundered. Withal many another doughty
baron was slain with them. But Desir,
together with his judges, and a great
multitude of the Lombards, fled away and
entered into Pavia ; and King Charles followed after them, and besieged the city on
all sides. Withal he sent into France for
his wife and his children. But the holy
Albins, bishop of Angier, and many other
bishops and abbots gave counsel to the
King and the Queen, that they should bury
the dead and make there a church : and
the said counsel pleased much the King,
and there were made two churches, one by
the commandment of Charles in honour of
St. Eusebius of Verceil, and the other by
the commandment of the Queen in honour
of St. Peter.

AND the King did do bear thither two
arks of stone, wherein were buried
Amis and Amile ; and Amile was borne
into the Church of St. Peter, and Amis into
the Church of St. Eusebius ; and the other
corpses were buried here and there. But

on the morrow's morn the body of Amile, *The*
and his coffin therewith, was found in the *Friend-*
Church of St. Eusebius hard by the coffin *ship of*
of Amis his fellow.   *Amis and*

NOW hear ye of this marvellous fellow- *Amile*
ship which might not be sundered by
death. This wonder wrought for them
God, who had given such might to His
disciples that they had power to move
mountains and shift them.   But because of
this miracle the King and the Queen abode
there thirty days, and did do the service of
them that were slain, and worshipped the
said churches with great gifts.

MEANWHILE, the host of Charles
wrought for the taking of the city
which they had besieged ; and our Lord
tormented them that were within in such
wise that they were brought to nought by
great feebleness and by mortalities.   And
after ten months from the time when the
city was besieged, Charles took Desir, and
all them who were with him, and laid the
city and all the realm under his subjection.
And King Desir and his wife they led into
France.

BUT Saint Albins, who by that time
had raised the dead to life, and given

light to many blind folk, ordained clerks,
priests, and deacons in the aforesaid Church
of St. Eusebius, and commanded them that
they should without ceasing guard and
keep the bodies of those two fellows, AMIS
and AMILE, who suffered death at the
hands of Desir, King of Lombardy, on the
fourth of the ides of October.

Reigning our Lord Jesus Christ, who
liveth and reigneth without end with the
Father and the Holy Ghost.   AMEN.

THE TALE OF KING FLORUS
AND THE FAIR JEHANE

HERE telleth the tale of a king who had to name King Florus of Ausay. A full good knight was he and a gentle- man of high lineage. The said King Florus of Ausay took to wife the daughter of the Prince of Brabant, who was a woman very gentle, and of great line : and a right fair maid was she when he wedded her and dainty of body and fashion ; and saith the tale that she was but of fifteen years when the King Florus took her, and he but of seventeen. A full good life they lived, as for young folk who loved together dearly : but King Florus might have no child of her, whereof he was sore grieving, and she also was exceeding heavy-hearted thereat. Much fair was this lady, and much she loved God and Holy Church, and there-with was so good almsgiver and so charit-able that she fed and clad poor people and kissed their feet. And to mesel folk both carles and queans was she so kind and careful, that the Holy Ghost dwelt in her. Her Lord King Florus went often to tournays in Alemain and France, and in many other lands whereas he wotted of them, when he was without war : much good he expended thereon and much honour he gained thereby.

BUT now leaveth the tale to tell of him and taketh up the word of a knight who dwelt in the marches of Flanders and Hainault. This said knight was full valiant and hardy, and right trusty, and had to wife a full fair dame of whom he had a much fair daughter, who had to name Jehane and was then of the age of twelve years. Much word there was of this fair maiden ; for in all the land was none so fair. Her mother spake often to her lord that he should give her in marriage ; but he was so given up to the following of tournays, that he was nowise hot on the wedding of his daughter, and his wife ever admonished him thereof when he came home from his tournays.

NOW this knight had a squire who had to name Robin, and was the valiantest squire to be found in any land, and by his prowess and his good fame oft he bore

away the prize for his lord from the tournay whereas he wended. Whereon it befel
that his lady thus bespake him : " Robin,
my lord is so given up to these tournays
that I know not how to speak with him,
whereof I am sore at heart, for I would
well that he should lay pain and care to the
wedding of my daughter ; wherefore I pray
thee, for the love of me, that whenas thou
seest the point thou say to him that he doth
very ill and is sore blamed that he weddeth
not his fair daughter, for there is no knight
in the land how rich soever he be who
would not take her with a good will."
" Lady," said Robin, " ye have said well ;
I will say it right well ; since forsooth he
troweth me of many things, and so will he
hereof meseemeth." " Robin," said the
lady, " I pray thee of this business for all
guerdon." " Dame," said Robin, " I am
well prayed hereof ; and wot ye that I will
do to my power herein." " It is enough,"
said the lady.

NO long while after the knight betook
him to wending to a tournay afar
from his land, and when he came there he
was retained straightway of the fellowship,
he and the knight of whose mesney he was,

and his banner was borne into the hostel of his lord. The tournay began, and the knight did so well by means of the good deeds of Robin, his squire, that he bore off the praise and prize of the tournay from one party and the other. On the second day the knight betook him to wending to his own land, and Robin put him to reason many times and blamed him much in that he gave not his fair daughter in marriage, and many times he said it to him, till at the last his lord said to him : "Robin, thou and thy lady give me no peace about the marrying of my daughter ; but as yet I know and see no man in my land unto whom I would give her." "Ah, sir," said Robin, "there is not a knight in thy land who would not take her with a good will." "Fair friend Robin, they are of no avail, all of them ; and to none of them shall I give her ; and forsooth to no one would I give her as now, save to one man only, and he forsooth is no knight." "Sir, tell me of him," said Robin, "and I shall speak or let speak to him so subtilly that the marriage shall be made." "Certes, Robin," said the knight, "from the semblance that I see of thee thou willest well that my

64

daughter should be wedded." "Sir," said *The Tale* Robin, "thou sayest sooth, for it is well *of King* time." "Robin," said the knight, "whereas *Florus* thou art so eager that my daughter should *and the* be wedded, she shall be wedded right soon *Fair* if thou accord to the said wedding." *Jehane* "Certes, sir," said Robin, "of a good will shall I accord thereto." "Wilt thou give me thy word herein?" "Yea, sir," said Robin. "Robin, thou hast served me exceeding well, and I have found thee a valiant man, and a loyal, and such as I be thou hast made me, and great gain have I gotten by thee, to wit, five hundred pounds of land; for it was but a little while that I had but five hundred, and now have I a thousand, and I tell thee that I owe much to thee: wherefore will I give my fair daughter unto thee, if thou wilt take her." "Ha, sir," said Robin, "God's mercy, what is this thou sayest? I am too poor a person to have so high a maiden, nor one so fair and so rich as my damsel is; I am not meet thereto. For there is no knight in this land, be he never so gentle a man, but would take her with a good will." "Robin, know that no knight of this land shall have her, but I shall give her to thee, if thou will it ; and thereto will I give thee four hundred pounds of my land." "Ha, sir," said Robin, "I deem that thou mockest me." "Robin," said the knight, "wot thou surely that I mock thee not." "Ha, sir, neither my lady nor her great lineage will accord hereto." "Robin," said the knight, "nought shall be done herein at the will of any of them. Hold! here is my glove, I invest thee with four hundred pounds of my land, and I will be thy warrant for all." "Sir," said Robin, "I will nought naysay it ; fair is the gift since I know that is soothfast." "Robin," said the knight, "now hast thou the rights thereof."

Then the knight delivered to him his glove, and invested him with the land and his fair daughter.

THEN rode the knight so far by his journeys, that he came into his land, and when he was come thither, his wife, who was a much fair lady, made him right great joy, and said to him : "Sir, for God's sake think of thy fair daughter, that she be wedded." "Dame," said the lord, "so much hast thou spoken hereof that I have wedded her." "Sir," said the lady, " unto

66

whom ?" "Forsooth, dame, I have given *The Tale*
her to such a man as shall never lack of *of King*
valiancy : I have given her to Robin my *Florus*
squire." "Robin ! Alas !" quoth the *and the*
lady ; "Robin hath nought, and there is *Fair*
no knight so mighty in all the land, but *Jehane*
will take her with a good will ; of a surety
Robin shall never have her." "Yea, but
have her he shall, dame," said the knight,
"and I have invested him with four
hundred pounds of my land ; and all that
I ought to warrant him, warrant him I
will." When the dame heard that, she
was much sorry, and said to her lord that
Robin should have her never. "Nay,
dame," said the lord, "have her he shall,
wilt thou or wilt thou not ; for even so
have I made covenant and I will hold to
the same."

WHEN the lady heard her lord, she
entered into her chamber and fell
a-weeping and making great dole ; after the
dole which she made she sent to seek her
brothers and her nephews and her cousins
germain, and showed them that which her
lord would do ; and they said to her :
"Dame, what will ye that we do ? We
have no will to go against thy lord, for he

is a knight valiant and hardy and weighty withal : and on the other hand he may do with his daughter according to his will, and with his land which he hath gotten withal. So wot thou well that we will not hang shield on neck herein." " Nay ? alas, then ! " said the dame, " so shall my heart never have joy if I lose my fair daughter. At least, fair lords, I pray you that ye show him that if he does thus he will neither do well nor according to his honour." " Dame," say they, " this setting forth will we do with a good will."

SO they came unto the knight, and when they had showed him their business he answered them right courteously : " Fair lords, I will tell you what I will do for the love of you ; if it please you I will put off the wedding in this wise as I shall tell you ; to wit : Amongst you ye be rich and of great lands ; ye are nigh friends of my fair daughter, whom I love much. If ye will give her four hundred pounds of land I will set aside the wedding, and she shall be wedded elsewhere according to your coun-sel." " A-God's name," quoth they, " we be nought fain to lay down so much." " Well, then," said the knight, " since ye

68

will not do this, then suffer me to do with my daughter as I list." "Sir, with a good will," said they.

S O the knight sent for his chaplain, and brought thither his fair daughter, and let affiance her to Robin, and set a day for the wedding. But the third day thereafter, Robin spake to his lord, and prayed him make him a knight, whereas it was nought meet that he should take to him so high a wife and so fair before he was a knight. His lord had great joy thereof, and the next day he was made knight, and the third day wedded the fair maiden with great feast and joyance.

B UT when master Robin was made knight he spake thus to his lord : "Sir, ye have made me knight ; and true it is that against the peril of death I vowed me to the road unto Saint Jamesward on the morrow of my knighting ; wherefore I pray thee take it not in dudgeon if to-morrow morn I must needs go my ways so soon as I shall have wedded thy fair daughter ; whereas in nowise will I break mine oath." "Forsooth, master Robin, if thou leave thus my fair daughter and thus wise go your ways, ye shall be much to blame." "Sir," said he, "I shall come back right soon if God will ; but this way-faring I needs must perforce." Whenas a certain knight of the court of the lord heard these words he blamed Sir Robin much, whereas he was leaving his fair wife at such a point, and Sir Robin said that he needs must do it. " Certes," said the knight, who had to name Raoul, "if thou goest thus to Saint James without touching thy fair wife, I will make thee cuckold before thine home-coming, and when thou comest home I will give thee good tokens that I have had share of her. Now I will lay my land thereto against thine, which our lord hath given thee, for I have well four hundred pounds of land even as thou hast." " Forsooth," said Sir Robin, "my wife is not come of such blood as that she shall misdo against me, and I may not believe in it nowise : I will make the wager with thee, if it please thee." " Yea," said Sir Raoul, " wilt thou pledge thee thereto ? " " Yea, verily," said Sir Robin, " and thou ? " " Yea, and I also. Now go we to my lord and make record of our covenant." " That will I well," said Sir Robin. Therewith they go

unto the lord, and the wager was recorded,
and they pledged them to hold thereto.
On the morrow betimes Sir Robin wedded
the fair maiden, and straightway after mass
was said, he departed from the house and
left the wedding, and took the road for St.
Jakem.

BUT now leaveth the tale to tell of him
and telleth of Sir Raoul, who was in
great imagination how he might win his
wager and lie by the fair lady. And saith
the tale that the lady held her much simply
while her lord was on pilgrimage, and was
going to the minster with a good will, and
prayed God that he would bring back her
lord. But Sir Raoul pained him on the
other hand how he might win his wager,
for great doubt he had to lose his land.
He spake with the carline who dwelt with
the fair lady, and said to her, that if she
could so bring it about that she might set
him in place and at point that he might
speak privily with my lady Jehane, and
have his will of her, he would give her
much good, so that there would be no
hour when she should not be rich. "Sir,
forsooth," said the carline, "thou art so
fair a knight, and so wise and courteous,

that my lady should well ought to love thee par amours, and I will put myself to the pain herein to the utmost of my might." Then the knight drew out straightway a forty sols, and gave it to her to buy a gown. The carline took them with a goodwill, and set them away surely, and said that she would speak with the lady. The knight departed from the carline, and the carline abode and took her lady to task when she came back from the minster, and said to her : " In God's name, lady, tell me true ! My lord, when he went to Saint Jakem, had he ever lain by thee ? " " Wherefore dost thou say this, dame Hersent ? " " Lady, because I trow that thou be yet a clean maid." " Certes, dame Hersent, so am I verily ; for of no woman wot I who would do such a deed." " Lady," said dame Hersent, " great damage it is ; for if ye wotted how great is the joy that women have when they be with a man who loveth them, ye would say that there is no joy so great ; and for this cause I marvel much that ye love not par amours even as these other ladies who all love. But if it pleaseth thee the matter is ready to hand ; whereas I wot of a

72

knight, fair and valiant and wise, who will *The Tale*
love thee with a good will ; a much rich *of King*
man is he, and fairer by far than the *Florus*
coward recreant who hath left thee. And *and the*
if ye dare love ye may have whatso ye *Fair*
dare ask ; and so much joy shall ye have *Jehane*
as never lady had more." So much spake
the carline by her words that the needle of
nature stirred somewhat. The lady asked
who the knight might be. "Who is it,
lady ? A-God's name ! I may well name
him. It is the lovely, the valiant, the
hardy Sir Raoul, who is one of the mesney
of thy father ; the kindest heart men wot
of." "Dame Hersent," said the lady,
"thou wert best let such words be ; for I
have no desire to misdo of my body, of no
such blood am I come." "Dame," said
the carline, "I wot well. But never shalt
thou know the worthy joy when a man
wendeth with a woman."

THUSWISE abode the matter. Sir
Raoul came back to the carline, and
she told him how she had talked with the
lady, and what she had answered. "Dame
Hersent," said the knight, "thus wise
should a good lady answer ; but ye shall
speak with her again, for one doeth not

73

*The Tale
of King
Florus
and the
Fair
Jehane*
the business at the first stroke : and hold, here be twenty sols to buy thee a cloth to thy surcoat." The carline took the silver, and spake with the lady often, but nought it availed.

WORE the time till at last they heard news that Sir Robin was wending back from Saint Jakem, and that he was already hard on Paris. Soon was known the tidings, and Sir Raoul, who had fear of the losing of his lands, returned to the carline, and spake with her ; and she said that she might not bring the business to an end : but that she would do so much for the love of him, if she should earn her service, that she would so bring it about as that there should be none in the house save he and this lady : and then he might do his will on her, will she nill she : and he said that he asked for nought else. "Then," said the carline, "ye, my lord, shall come within eight days, and I will do my lady to bathe her in her chamber, and I will send all the mesney out of the house and out of the castle ; then can ye come to her bathing in the chamber, and may have your desire of her, either with her good will or maugre." "Ye have well said," quoth he.

74

ABODE matters thus till Sir Robin sent *The Tale* word that he was coming to hand, *of King* and would be at the house on the Sunday. *Florus* Then the carline let bathe the lady the *and the* Thursday before, and the bath was in her *Fair* chamber, and the fair lady entered therein. *Jehane* But the carline sent after Sir Raoul, and he came. Thereafter she sent all the folk of the household out of the house. Sir Raoul came his ways to the chamber and entered therein, and greeted the lady, but she greeted him not again, but said thus : "Sir Raoul, thou art nowise courteous. Whether wottest thou forsooth that it is well with me of thy coming? accursed be thou, villain knight!" But Sir Raoul said : "My lady, mercy, a-God's name! I am but dying for grief of thee. For God's sake have pity of me!" "Sir Raoul," said she, "I will have no mercy in such wise that I will ever be thy darling. And wot thou well that if thou leave me not in peace I will tell my lord, my father, the honour thou requirest of me : for I am none such as that." "Nay, lady, is it so, then?" "Yea, verily," said she.

THEREWITH Sir Raoul drew nigh to her, and embraced her in his arms,

75

which were strong enow, and drew her all naked out of the bath and bore her toward her bed ; and so soon as he drew her forth of the bath he saw a black spot which she had on her right groin hard by her natural part ; and he thought therewithal that that were a good token that he had lain by her. Thus as he bore her off to her bed, his spurs hooked them into the serge at the bed's edge toward the foot thereof, and down fell the knight, he and the lady together, he below and she above ; but she rose up straightway and caught up a billet of wood, and smote Sir Raoul therewith amidst the face, and made him a wound both deep and wide, so that the blood fell to earth. So when Sir Raoul felt himself hurt he had no great desire to play, wherefore he arose and got him gone out of the chamber straightway : he did so much that he came to his hostel, where he dwelt a good league thence, and there he had his wound dealt with. But the good dame entered into her bath again, and called dame Hersent, and told the adventure of the knight.

MUCH great array made the father of the fair lady against the coming of

Sir Robin, and he summoned much folk, and sent and bade Sir Raoul to come ; but he sent word that he might not come, for that he was sick. On the Sunday came Sir Robin, and was received right fairly ; and the father of the fair lady went to seek Sir Raoul and found him wounded, and said that now for nought might he abide behind from the feast. So he dight his face and his hurt the best wise he might, and went to the feast, which was great and grand day long of drinking and of eating, and of dancing and carolling.

WHEN night was come Sir Robin went to bed with his wife, who received him much joyously as a good dame ought to her lord ; so abode they in joy and in feast the more part of the night. On the morrow great was the feast, and the victual was dight and they ate. But when it was after dinner, Sir Raoul bore on hand Sir Robin, and said that he had won his land, whereas he had known his wife carnally, by the token, to wit, that she had a black spot on her right thigh and a pearlet hard by her jewel. "Thereof I wot not," said Sir Robin, "for I have not looked on her so close." "Well, then,

77

I tell thee," said Sir Raoul, "by the oath that thou hast given me that thou take heed thereof, and do me right." "So will I, verily," said Sir Robin.

WHEN night was, Sir Robin played with his wife, and found and saw on her right thigh the black spot, and a pearlet hard by her fair jewel : and when he knew it he was sore grieving. On the morrow he went to Sir Raoul, and said before his lord that he had lost his wager. Heavy of heart was he day long, and when it was night he went to the stable, and set the saddle on his palfrey, and went forth from the house, bearing with him what he might get him of silver. So came to Paris, and when he was at Paris he abode there three days. But now leaveth the tale to tell of him, and taketh up the word concerning his wife.

HERE saith the tale that much sorrowful was the fair lady and heavy of heart, when she called to mind how she had cast her lord out of his house. Much she thought of the wherefore thereof and wept and made great dole ; till her father came to her, and said that he were fainer if she were yet to wed, whereas she had done

78

him shame and all them of his lineage ;
and he told her how and wherefore. When
she heard that, she was sore grieved and
denied the deed downright ; but nought
availed. For it is well known that shame
so sore is contrary to all women, that if a
woman were to burn all, she would not be
trowed of such a misdoing, once it were
laid on her.

ON the first hour of the night the lady
arose, and took all pennies that she
had in her coffer, and took a nag and a
harness thereto, and gat her to the road ;
and she had let shear her fair tresses, and
was otherwise arrayed like to an esquire.
So much she went by her journeys that
she came to Paris, and went after her
lord ; and she said and declared that she
would never make an end before she had
found him. Thus she rode like to a
squire. And on a morning she went
forth out of Paris, and wended the way
toward Orleans until she came to the
Tomb Isory, and there she fell in with her
lord Sir Robin. Full fain she was when
she saw him, and she drew up to him and
greeted him, and he gave her greeting
back and said : " Fair friend, God give

79

thee joy!" "Sir," said she, "whence art thou?" "Forsooth, fair friend, I am of old Hainault." "Sir, whither wendeth thou?" "Forsooth, fair friend, I wot not right well whither I go, nor where I shall dwell. Forsooth, needs must I where fortune shall lead me; and she is contrary enough; for I have lost the thing in the world that most I ever loved: and she also hath lost me. Withal I have lost my land, which was great and fair enough. But what hast thou to name, and whither doth God lead thee?" "Certes, sir," said Jehane, "I am minded for Marseilles on the sea, where is war as I hope. There would I serve some valiant man, about whom I shall learn me arms if God will. For I am so undone in mine own country that therein for a while of time I may not have peace. But, sir, meseemeth that thou be a knight, and I would serve thee with a right good will if it please thee. And of my company wilt thou be nought worsened." "Fair friend," said Sir Robin, "a knight am I verily. And where I may look to find war, thitherward would I draw full willingly. But tell me what thou hast to name?"

80

"Sir," said she, "I have to name John." *The Tale*
"In a good hour," quoth the knight. *of King*
"And thou, sir, how hight thou?" "John," *Florus*
said he, "I have to name Robin." "Sir *and the*
Robin, retain me as thine esquire, and I *Fair*
will serve thee to my power." "John, so *Jehane*
would I with a good will. But so little of
money have I that I must needs sell my
horse before three days are worn. Wherefore I wot not how to do to retain thee."
"Sir," said John, "be not dismayed thereof,
for God will aid thee if it please him. But
tell me where thou wilt eat thy dinner?"
"John, my dinner will soon be made; for
not another penny have I than three sols of
Paris." "Sir," said John, "be nought
dismayed thereof, for I have hard on ten
pounds Tournais, whereof thou shalt not
lack, if thou hast not to spend at thy will."
"Fair friend John, have thou mickle
thanks."

THEN made they good speed to Montl-
hery: there John dight meat for his
lord and they ate. When they had eaten,
the knight slept in a bed and John at his
feet. When they had slept, John did on
the bridles, and they mounted and gat to
the road. They went so far by their

F   81

journeys that they came to Marseilles-on-Sea ; but of war they heard no word there, whereof were they much sorry. But now leaveth the tale to tell of them two, and returneth to tell of Sir Raoul, who had by falsehood gained the land of Sir Robin.

HERE telleth the tale that so long did Sir Raoul hold the land of Sir Robin without righteous cause, for seven years' wearing. Then he took a great sickness and of that sickness was sore beaten down, insomuch that he was on the point of death. Now he doubted much the transgression which he had done against the fair lady the daughter of his lord, and against her husband also, whereby they were undone, both of them by occasion of his malice. Exceeding ill at ease was he of his wrongdoing, which was so great that he durst not confess it.

CAME a day when he was sore undone by his sickness, so he sent for his chaplain whom he loved much, for he had found him a man valiant and loyal ; and he said to him : "Sir, thou who art my father before God, know that I look to die of this sickness, wherefore I pray thee for God's sake that ye aid me with your counsel, for great is my need thereof, for I have done *The Tale* an ill deed so hideous and dark that scarce *of King* shall I have mercy therefor." The chaplain *Florus* bade him tell it out hardily, and that he *and the* would aid him with counsel to his power; *Fair* till at last Sir Raoul told him all as ye have *Jehane* heard afore. And he prayed him for God's sake give him counsel, so great as was his mis-doing. "Sir," said he, "be nought dismayed, for if thou wilt do the penance which I enjoin thee, I will take thy transgression on me and on my soul, so that thou shalt be quit." "Yea, tell me then," said the knight. "Sir," said he, "thou shalt take the cross far over sea, and thou shalt get thee thereto within the year wherein thou art whole, and shalt give pledges to God that thou shalt so do : and in every place where men ask thee the occasion of thy journey, thou shalt tell it to all who shall ask it of thee." "All this will I well do," said the knight. "Then, sir, give thou good pledge." "With a good will," said the knight ; "thou thyself shalt abide surety for me, and I swear to thee on my knighthood that I shall quit thee well." "A-God's name, sir !" quoth the chaplain, "I will be thy surety." Now turned the knight to amendment, and was all whole ;

and a year wore wherein he went not over sea. The chaplain spake to him often thereof, but he held the covenant as but a jest ; till at last the chaplain said that but if he acquitted him before God of his pledge, he would tell the tale to the father of the fair damsel, who had been thus undone by him. When the knight heard that, he said to the chaplain that within half a year he would set about the crossing of the sea, and so swore to him. But now leaveth the tale to tell of the knight, and returneth to telling of King Florus of Ausaye, of whom for a great while it hath been silent.

NOW saith the tale that a much good life led King Florus of Ausay and his wife, as of young folk who loved each other ; but much sorry and heavy-hearted were they that they might have no child. The lady made great prayers to God, and let sing masses ; but whereas it was not well pleasing to God, it might not be. But on a day came thither into the house of King Florus a good man who had his dwelling in the great forest of Ausaye in a place right wild ; and when the queen knew that he was come she came unto him and made him right great joy. And because he was

84

a good man she confessed to him and told him all her ailing, and how that she was ex- ceeding heavy of heart, because she had had no child by her lord. " Ah, lady," said the good man, " since it pleaseth not our Lord, needs must thou abide it ; and when it pleaseth him thou shalt have one, or two." " Certes, sir," said the lady, " I were fain thereof ; for my lord holdeth me the less dear, and the high barons of this land also. Withal it hath been told to me that they have spoken to my lord to leave me and take another." " Verily, dame," said the good man, " he would do ill ; it would be done against God and against Holy Church." " Ah, sir, I pray thee to pray to God for me that I may have a child of my lord, for great fear I have lest he leave me." "Dame," said the good man, " my prayer shall avail but little, but if it please God ; neverthe- less I will pray heartily."

THE good man departed from the lady, and the barons of the land and of the country came to the King Florus, and bade him send away his wife and take another, since by this he might have no child. And if he did not after their counsel, they would go and dwell otherwhere ; for in no case would they that the realm should be without an heir. King Florus feared his barons and trowed their word, and he said that he would send away his wife, and that they should seek him another, and they trusted him therein. When the lady knew it she was exeeeding heavy of heart ; but nought durst she do, for she knew that her lord would leave her. So she sent for the hermit who had been her confessor, and he came to her. Then the lady told him all the tale of the matter of the barons, who would seek for their lord another woman. "And I pray thee, good father, that thou wouldst aid me, and counsel me what I should do." " Dame," said the good man, "if it be so as thou sayest, ye must needs suffer it ; for against thy lord and against his barons ye may do nought perforce." " Sir," said the good lady, " thou sayest sooth : but if it please God, I were fain to be a recluse nigh unto thee ; whereby I may be at the service of God all the days of my life, and that I may have comfort of thee." " Dame," said the good man, " that would be over strange a thing, whereas thou art too young a lady and too fair. But I will tell thee what thou shalt do. Hard by my hermitage there is an abbey of White Nuns, who are right good ladies, and I counsel you go thither ; and they will have great joy of thee for thy goodness and thy high dignity." "Sir," said she, "thou hast well said ; I will do all that thou counsellest me."

ON the morrow King Florus spake to his wife, and said thus : "Needs must thou and I sunder, for that thou mayst have no child by me. Now I say thee soothly that the sundering lies heavy on me, for never shall I love woman as I have loved thee." Therewith fell King Florus to weep sorely, and the lady also. "Sir," said she, "a-God's mercy ! And whither shall I go, and what shall I do ?" "Dame, thou shalt do well, if it please God, for I will send thee back well and richly into thy country to thy kindred." "Sir," said the lady, "it shall not be so : I have purveyed me an abbey of nuns, where I will be, if it please thee ; and there I will serve God all my life ; for since I lose thy company I am she that no man shall go with any more." Thereat King Florus wept and the lady also. But on the third day the queen went to the abbey ; and the other queen was come, and had great feast made her, and great joy of

*The Tale
of King
Florus
and the
Fair
Jehane*
her friends. King Florus held her for three
years, but never might have child of her.
But here the tale holdeth peace of King
Florus, and betaketh it again to Sir Robin,
and to John who were at Marseilles.

HERE telleth the tale that much sorry
was Sir Robin when he came to
Marseilles, whereas he heard tell of nought
toward in the country ; so he said to John :
" What do we ? Thou hast lent me of thy
moneys, whereof I thank thee : I will
give them back to thee, for I will sell
my palfrey, and quit me toward thee."
" Sir," said John, " if it please thee, believe
me, and I shall tell thee what we shall do.
I have yet well an hundred sols of Tournay,
and if it please thee, I will sell our two
horses, and make money thereby : for I am
the best of bakers that ye may wot of ; and
I will make French bread, and I doubt me
not but I shall earn my spending well and
bountifully."   " John," said Sir Robin,
" I grant it thee to do all as thou
wilt."

SO on the morrow John sold the two horses
for ten pounds Tournays, and bought
corn and let grind it, and bought baskets, and
fell to making French bread, so good and so
88

well made that he sold it for more than the *The Tale*
best baker of the town might do ; and he *of King*
did so much within two years that he had *Florus*
well an hundred pounds of chattels. Then *and the*
said John to his lord : "I rede thee well that *Fair*
we buy us a very great house, and that we *Jehane*
buy us wine and take to harbouring good
folk." "John," said Sir Robin, "do
according to thy will, for I grant it thee,
and moreover I praise thee much." So
John bought a house, great and fair, and
harboured good folk, and earned enough
plenteously ; and he arrayed his lord well
and richly ; and Sir Robin had his palfrey,
and went to eat and drink with the most
worthy of the town, and John sent him
wine and victual, so that all they that
haunted his company marvelled thereat.
So much he gained that in three years' time
he had gotten him more than three hundred
pounds of garnishment, out-taken his plenishing, which was well worth fifty pounds.
But here leaveth the tale to tell of Sir Robin
and of John, and goeth back to tell of Sir
Raoul.
FOR, saith the tale, that the chaplain
held Sir Raoul right short that he should
go over sea, and quit him of the pledge he

had laid down ; for great fear he had lest he yet should leave it ; and so much he did that Sir Raoul saw well that he needs must go. So he dight his journey, and arrayed him right richly, as he that hath well enough thereto ; and so he betook him to the road with three squires : and went so much by his journeys that he came into Marseilles-on-sea and took lodging in the French hostel, whereas dwelt Sir Robin and John. So soon as John saw him she knew him by the scar of the wound she had made him, and because she had seen him many times. The knight sojourned in the town fifteen days, and hired him passage. But the while he sojourned, John drew him in to privy talk, and asked of him the occasion of his going over sea, and Sir Raoul told him all the occasion, as one who had little heed thereof, even as the tale hath told afore. When John heard that, he held his peace. Sir Raoul set his goods aboard ship, and went upon the sea ; but tarried so much the ship wherein he was that he abode in the town for eight days ; but on the ninth day he betook him to go his ways to the holy sepulchre, and did his pilgrimage, and confessed him the best he might : and his

90

confessor charged him in penance that he *The Tale* should give back the land which he held *of King* wrongfully to the knight and his wife. *Florus* Whereon he said to his confessor, that *and the* when he came into his own country he *Fair* would do what his heart bade him. So he *Jehane* departed from Jerusalem and came to Acre, and dight his passage as one who had great longing to repair to his own country. He went up on to the sea, and wended so diligently, as well by night as by day, till in less than three months he came to the port of Aigues-mort. Then he departed from the port and came straight to Marseilles, wherein he sojourned eight days in the hostel of Sir Robin and John, which hight the French house. Never did Sir Robin know him, for on that matter he thought nothing. At the end of eight days he departed from Marseilles, he and his squires, and went so long by his journeys that he came into his own country, where he was received with great joy, as one who was a knight rich in land and chattels. Thereon his chaplain took him to task, and asked of him if any had demanded the occasion of his journey; and he said: "Yea, in three places, to wit: Marseilles, Acre, and Jerusalem : and he of whom I took counsel bade me to give back the land to Sir Robin, if I hear tidings of him, or to his wife else, or to his heir." "Certes," said the chaplain ; "he bade thee good counsel." Thus was Sir Raoul in his own country a great while in rest and good ease. But here leaveth the tale to tell of him, and returneth to Sir Robin and John.

HERE saith the tale that when Sir Robin and John had been at Marseilles for six years that John had gotten to the value of six hundred pounds, and they were come into the seventh year, and John might gain eke what he would, and so sweet he was, and so debonaire that he made himself loved of all the neighbours, and therewithal he was of good hap as he might not be of more, and maintained his lord so nobly and so richly that it was wonder to behold. When the end of the seven years drew nigh, John fell to talk with his lord Sir Robin, and spake thus : "Sir, we have now been a great while in this country, and so much have we gained, that we have hard on six hundred pounds of chattels, what of money, what of vessel of silver." "Forsooth, John," said Sir Robin, "they be not *The Tale* mine, but thine ; for it is thou hast earned *of King* them." "Sir," said John, "saving thy *Florus* grace, it is not so, but they are thine : for *and the* thou art my rightful lord, and never, if it *Fair* please God, will I change." "Gramercy, *Jehane* John, I hold thee not for servant, but for companion and friend." "Sir," said John, "all days I have kept thee loyal company, and shall do from henceforth." "By my faith," said Sir Robin, "I will do what so pleaseth thee : but to go into my country, I wot not to say thereof : for I have lost so much there that hardly shall my scathe be righted to me." "Sir," said John, "be thou never dismayed of that matter ; for when thou art come into thine own country thou shalt hear good tidings, please God. And doubt thou nothing, for in all places whereas we shall be, if it please God, I shall earn enough for thee and for me." "Certes, John," said Sir Robin, "I will do as it pleaseth thee, and where thou wilt that I go, thither will I." "Sir," said John, "I shall sell our chattels, and dight our journey, and we will go within fifteen days." "A-God's name, John," said Sir Robin.

J OHN sold all his plenishing, whereof he had good store and goodly, and bought three horses, a palfrey for his lord, another for himself, and a sumpter horse. Then they took leave of the neighbours, and the most worthy of the town, who were sore grieved of their departure.

W ORE the way Sir Robin and John, insomuch that in three weeks' space they came into their country. And Robin made known to his lord, whose daughter he had had, that he was at hand. The lord was much joyful thereof, for he was deeming well that his daughter would be with him. And she indeed it was, but in the guise of an esquire. Sir Robin was well received of his lord, whose daughter he had erewhile wedded. When the lord could have no tidings of his daughter, he was right sorrowful; nevertheless he made good feast to Sir Robin, and bade thereto his knights and his neighbours ; and thither came Sir Raoul, who held the land of Sir Robin wrongfully. Great was the joy that day and the morrow, and that while Sir Robin told to John the occasion of the wager, and how Sir Raoul held his land wrongfully. "Sir," said John, "do thou

94

appeal him of treason, and I will do the battle for thee." "Nay, John," said Sir Robin, "thou shalt not do it."

SO they left it till the morrow, when John came to Sir Robin and did him to wit that he would speak to the father of his wife ; and thus he said to him : "Sir, thou art lord to my lord Sir Robin after God, and he wedded thy daughter time was. But there was a wager betwixt him and Sir Raoul, who said that he would make him cuckold by then he returned from St. Jakeme; whereof Sir Raoul hath made false report, whereas he hath had nor part nor lot in thy fair daughter. And he hath done disloyal treason. All which things I am ready to prove on his body." Then leapt forth Sir Robin and said : "John, fair friend, none shall do the battle save I ; nowise shalt thou hang shield on neck herein." Therewith Sir Robin reached his pledge to his lord ; and Sir Raoul was sore grieving of the pledging, but needs must he defend him, or cry craven ; so he reached for this pledge right cowardly. So were the pledges given, and day of battle appointed on that day fifteen days without naysay.

NOW hear ye marvels of John what he did. John who had to name my Lady Jehane, had in the house of her father a cousin germain of hers, who was a fair damsel, and of some five and twenty years. Jehane came to her, and laid all the whole truth bare to her, and told her the whole business from point to point, and showed her all openly ; and prayed her much that she would hide all the matter until the time and hour came when she should make herself known to her father. Wherefore her cousin, who knew her well, said to her that she would keep all well hidden, so that by her it should never be discovered. Then was the chamber of her cousin dight for the Lady Jehane ; and the said lady, the while of the fortnight before the battle should be, let bathe her and stove her ; and she took her ease the best she might, as one who well had therewithal. And she let cut and shape for her duly four pair of gowns, of Scarlet, of Vair, of Perse, and of cloth of silk ; and she took so well her ease that she came back to her most beauty, and was so fair and dainty as no lady might be more.

BUT when it came to the end of the fifteen days, then was Sir Robin sore

grieving of John his esquire, because he had
lost him, and knew not where he was
become. But none the more did he leave
to apparel him for the fight as one who had
heart enough and hardihood.

O N the morn of the day whenas the
battle was appointed, came both the
knights armed. They drew apart one
from the other, and then they fell on each
other with the irons of their glaives, and
smote on each other with so great heat that
they bore down each other's horses to the
earth beneath their bodies. Sir Raoul was
hurt a little on the left side. Sir Robin
rose up the first, and came a great pace on
Sir Raoul, and smote him a great stroke on
the helm in such wise that he beat down
the head-piece and drave in the sword on
to the mail-coif, and sheared all thereto ;
but the coif was of steel so strong that he
wounded him not, howbeit he made him to
stagger, so that he caught hold of the
arson of the saddle ; and if he had not, he
had fallen to earth. Then Sir Raoul, who
was a good knight, smote Sir Robin so
great a stroke upon the helm that he all to
astonied him ; and the stroke fell down to
the shoulder, and sheared the mails of the

G 97

hawberk, but hurt him not. Then Sir Robin smote him with all his might, but he threw his shield betwixt, and Sir Robin smote off a quarter thereof. When Sir Raoul felt his strong strokes, he misdoubted him much, and wished well that he were over sea, if he were but quit of the battle, and Sir Robin back on the land which he held. Nevertheless he put forth all his might and drew nigh, and fell on Sir Robin much hardly, and gave him a great stroke upon his shield so that he sheared it to the boss thereof. But Sir Robin laid a great stroke upon his helm, but he threw his shield betwixt and Sir Robin sheared it amidst, and the sword fell upon the neck of the horse, and sheared it amidst, and beat down straightway both horse and man. Then Sir Raoul leapt to his feet, as one who was in a stour exceeding heavy. Then Sir Robin lighted down, whereas he would not betake him to his horse while the other was afoot.

NOW were both knights come unto the skirmish and they hewed in pieces each other's shields and helms and hawberks, and drew the blood from each other's bodies with their trenchant swords; and

had they smitten as great strokes as at first, *The Tale*
soon had they slain each other, for they had *of King*
so little of their shields that scarce might *Florus*
they cover their fists therewith. Yet had *and the*
neither of them fear of death or shame : *Fair*
nevertheless the nighness of them to each *Jehane*
other called on them to bring the battle to
an end. Sir Robin took his sword in both
hands, and smote Sir Raoul with all his
might on the helm, and sheared it amidst,
so that one half thereof fell upon the shoul-
ders, and he sheared the steel coif, and
made him a great wound on the head; and
Sir Raoul was so astonied of the stroke
that he bent him to the earth on one knee;
but he rose up straightway and was in great
misease when he thus saw his head naked,
and great fear of death he had. But he
came up to Sir Robin and fetched a stroke
with all his might on what he had of shield
and he sheared it asunder and the stroke
came on the helm and cut into it well three
fingers, so that the sword came on the iron
coif, which was right good, so that the
sword brake a-twain. When Sir Raoul saw
his sword broken and his head naked, he
doubted much the death. Nevertheless he
stooped down to the earth, and took up a

99

great stone in his two hands, and cast it after Sir Robin with all his might ; but Sir Robin turned aside when he saw the stone coming, and ran on Sir Raoul, who took to flight all over the field ; and Sir Robin said to him that he would slay him but if he cried craven. Whereon Sir Raoul thus bespake him :

HAVE mercy on me, gentle knight, and lo here my sword, so much as I have thereof, and I render it to thee, and all of me therewith unto thy mercy ; and I pray thee have pity of me, and beg of thy lord and mine to have mercy on me and that thou and he save my life, and I render and give both thy land and mine. For I have held it against right and against reason. And I have wrongfully defamed the fair lady and good.

WHEN Sir Robin heard this, he said that he had done enough, and he prayed his lord so much that he pardoned Sir Raoul of his misdeed, in such wise that he was quit thereof on the condition that he should go over seas and abide there lifelong.

THUSWISE conquered Sir Robin his land and the land of Sir Raoul to boot

for all his days. But he was so sore griev- *The Tale*
ing and sad at heart of his good dame and *of King*
fair, whom he had thus lost, that he could *Florus*
have no solace ; and on the other hand, he *and the*
was so sore grieving for John his esquire *Fair*
whom he had so lost, that marvel it was. *Jehane*
And his lord was no less sad at heart for
his fair daughter whom he had thus lost,
and of whom he might have no tidings.

BUT dame Jehane, who was in the
chamber of her cousin germain for
fifteen days in good ease, when she wotted
that her lord had vanquished the battle, was
exceeding much at ease. Now she had
done make four pair of gowns, as is aforesaid, and she clad her with the richest of
them, which was of silk bended of fine gold
of Araby. Moreover she was so fair of
body and of visage, and so dainty withal,
that nought in the world might be found
fairer, so that her cousin germain all marvelled at her great beauty. And she had
been bathed, and attired and had ease at all
points for the fifteen days, so that she was
come into so great beauty as wonder was.
Much fair was the Lady Jehane in her
gown of silk bended of gold. So she called
her cousin to her and said : " How deemest

thou of me ? " " What, dame ! " said her cousin, " thou art the fairest lady of the world." " I shall tell thee, then, fair cousin, what thou shalt do : go thou tell so much before my father as that he shall make dole no more, but be glad and joyful, and that thou bearest him good news of his daughter who is whole and well ; and that he come with thee and thou wilt show him. Then bring him hither, and meseemeth he will see me with a good will." The damsel said that she would well do that errand ; and she came to the father of the Lady Jehane, and said him what his daughter had said. When her sire heard thereof great wonder he wist it, and went with the damsel, and found his daughter in her chamber, and knew her straightway, and put his arms about her neck, and wept over her for joy and pity, and had so great joy that scarce might he speak to her. Then he asked her where she had been so long a while. " Fair father," said she, " thou shalt know it well anon. But a-God's sake do my lady mother to come to me, for I have great longing to see her." The lord sent for his wife, and when she came into the chamber where was her daughter, and saw her and

knew her, she swooned for joy, and might *The Tale*
not speak a great while, and when she came *of King*
out of her swooning none might believe the *Florus*
great joy that she made of her daughter. *and the*

BUT whiles they were in this joy, the *Fair*
father of the fair lady went to seek Sir *Jehane*
Robin and bespake him thus : "Sir Robin,
fair sweet son, tidings can I say thee exceeding joyous us between." "Certes,"
said Sir Robin, "of joy have I great need,
for none save God can set rede to it whereby I may have joy. For I have lost thy
fair daughter, whereof have I sore grief at
heart. And thereto have I lost the swain
and the squire, who of all in the world hath
done me most good ; to wit, John the
good, my squire." "Sir Robin," said the
lord, "be ye nought dismayed thereof, for
of squires thou shalt find enough. But of
my fair daughter I could tell thee good
tidings ; for I have seen her e'en now ;
and, wot ye well, she is the fairest lady that
may be in the world." When Sir Robin
heard that, he trembled all with joy and
said to his lord : "Ah, sir, for God's sake
bring me where I may see if this be true !"
"With a good will," said the lord ; "come
along now."

THE lord went before and he after, till they were come to the chamber, where the mother was yet making great feast of her daughter, and they were weeping with joy one over the other. But when they saw their rightful lords a-coming, they rose up ; and so soon as Sir Robin knew his wife, he ran to her with his arms spread abroad, and they clipped and kissed together dearly, and wept of joy and pity ; and they were thus embracing together for the space of the running of ten acres, or ever they might sunder. Then the lord commanded the tables to be laid for supper, and they supped and made great joy.

AFTER supper, when the feast had been right great, they went to bed, and Sir Robin lay that night with the Lady Jehane his wife, who made him great joy, and he her in likewise ; and they spake together of many things, and so much that Sir Robin asked of her where she had been ; and she said : " Sir, long were it to tell, but thou shalt know it well in time. Now tell to me what thou couldest to do, and where thou hast been so long a while." " Lady," said Sir Robin, " that will I well tell thee."

104

S O he fell to telling her all that she well knew, and of John his esquire, who had done him so much good, and said that he was so troubled whereas he had thus lost him, that he would make never an end of wandering till he had found him, and that he would bestir himself thereto the morrow's morn. "Sir," said the lady, "that were folly ; and how should it be then ; wouldst thou leave me, then ? " "Forsooth, dame," said he, " e'en so it behoveth me. For none did ever so much for another as he did for me." "Sir," said the dame, "wherein he did for thee, he did but duly. Even so he was bound to do." "Dame," said Sir Robin, "by what thou sayest thou shouldst know him." "Forsooth," said the lady, "I should ought to know him well, for never did he anything whereof I wotted not." "Lady," said Sir Robin, "thou makest me to marvel at thy words." "Sir," said the lady, "never marvel thou hereof ! If I tell thee a word for sooth and for certain, wilt thou not believe me ? " "Dame," said he, " yea, verily."

"W ELL, then, believe me in this," said she ; "for wot of a verity that I am the very same John whom thou

*The Tale
of King
Florus
and the
Fair
Jehane* wouldest go seek, and I will tell thee how.
For I knew that thou wert gone for the
great sorrow thou hadst for my misdoing
against thee, and for thy land which thou
deemedst thou hadst lost for ever.   Whereas I had heard tell of the occasion of the
wager, and of the treason Sir Raoul had
done, whereof I was so wroth as never
woman was more wroth.   Straightway I
let shear my hair, and took the money in
my coffer, about ten pounds of Tournais,
and arrayed me like an esquire, and followed thee away to Paris, and found
thee at the tomb of Ysore ; and there I
fell into company with thee, and we
went together into Marseilles, and were
there together seven years long, where I
served thee unto my power as my rightful lord, and I hold for well spent all
the service that I did thee.   And know
of a truth that I am innocent and just
of that which the evil knight laid upon
me ; as well appeareth whereas he hath
been shamed in the field, and hath ac-
knowledged the treason."

THEREWITH my lady Jehane embraced Sir Robin, her lord, and kissed
him on the mouth right sweetly ; for Sir

Robin understood well that it was she that *The Tale*
had so well served him ; and so great joy *of King*
he had, that none could say it or think it ; *Florus*
and much he wondered in his heart how *and the*
she could think to do that which so turned *Fair*
to her great goodness.   Wherefore he loved *Jehane*
her the more all the days of his life.

THUS were these two good persons together ; and they went to dwell upon
their land, which they had both wide and
fair.   Good life they led as for young folk
who loved dearly together.   Sir Robin
went often to tournays with his lord, of
whose mesney he was, and much worship
he won, and great prize he conquered and
great wealth, and did so much that he gat
him as much land again as he had had.
And when the lord and his lady were dead,
then had he all the land.   And he did so
well by his prowess that he was made a
double banneret, and he had well four
thousand pounds of land.   But never might
he have child by his wife, whereof he was
much grieved.   Thus was he with his wife
for ten years after he had conquered the
battle with Sir Raoul.

AFTER the term of ten years, by the
will of God, to whom we be all sub-

ject, the pain of death took hold of him, and he died like a valiant man, and had all his rights, and was laid in earth with great worship. His wife the fair lady made so great sorrow over him, that all they that saw her had pity of her ; but in the end needs must she forget her mourning and take comfort, for as little as it were. Much abode the lady in her widowhood as a good dame and a holy, for she loved much God and Holy Church. She held her much humbly and much she loved the poor, and did them much good, and was so good a lady that none knew how to blame her or to say of her aught save great good. Therewithal was she so fair, that each one said who saw her, that she was the mirror of all ladies in the world for beauty and goodness. But here leaveth the tale a little to speak of her, and returneth to tell of the King Florus, of whom it hath been silent a great while.

FOR saith the tale, that King Florus of Ausay was in his own country sore grieving, and ill at ease for the departure of his first wife. Notwithstanding the other was brought unto him, and was both fair and dainty, but he could not hold her in

108

his heart like as he did the first one. Four
years was he with her, but never child
might he have of her ; and when the said
time was ended the pains of death took the
lady, and she was buried, whereof her
friends were sore grieving. But service
was done unto her, as was meet to a
queen.

THEN abode King Florus in widowhood more than two years, and he was
still a young man, whereas he was not of
more than five-and-forty winters, wherefore the barons said to him that he behoved
to marry again. " Forsooth," said King
Florus, " so to do have I no great longing,
for two wives have I had, and never child
might I have by either. And on the other
hand, the first that I had was so good and
so fair, and so much I loved her in my
heart for the great beauty that was in her,
that I may not forget her. And I tell you
well that never woman will I wed but I
may have her as fair and as good as was
she. Now may God have mercy on her
soul, for she hath passed away in the abbey
where she was, as folk have done me to
wit." " Ha, sir," said a knight, who was
of his privy counsel, "there be many good

dames up and down the country side, of whom ye know not all ; and I know one who hath not for goodness and beauty her peer in the world. And if thou knew her goodness, and saw but her beauty, thou wouldst say well that happy were the king who held the danger of such a lady. And wot well that she is a gentle lady, and valiant, and rich, and of great lands. And I will tell thee a part of her goodness so please thee."

SO the king said that he would well he should tell him. Wherefore the knight fell to telling how she had bestirred her to go seek her lord, and how she found him and brought him to Marseilles, and the great goodness and great services which she did him, even as the tale hath told afore, so that King Florus wondered much thereat ; and he said to the knight privily that such a woman he would take with a good will.

"SIR," said the knight, who was of the country of the lady, " I will go to her, if it please thee, and I will so speak to her, if I may, that the marriage of you two shall be made." " Yea," said King Florus, " I will well that thou go, and I pray thee to give good heed to the business."

SO the knight bestirred him, and went so much by his journeys that he came to the country where dwelt the fair dame, whom the tale calleth my Lady Jehane, and found her abiding at a castle of hers, and she made him great joy, as one whom she knew. The knight drew her to privy talk, and told her of King Florus of Ausay, how he bade her come unto him that he might take her to wife. When the lady heard the knight so speak, she began to smile, which beseemed her right well, and she said to the knight : "Thy king is neither so well learned, nor so courteous as I had deemed, whereas he biddeth me come to him and he will take me to wife : forsooth, I am no wageling of him to go at his command. But say to thy king, that, so please him, he come to me, if he prize me so much and loveth me, and it seem good to him that I take him to husband and spouse, for the lords ought to beseech the ladies, and not ladies the lords." "Lady," said the knight, "all that thou hast said to me, I will tell him straight ; but I doubt that he hold not with pride."

111

The Tale
of King
Florus
and the
Fair
Jehane

" Sir knight," said the lady, " he shall take
what heed thereof may please him : but in
the matter whereof I have spoken to thee,
he hath neither courtesy nor reason."
" Lady," said the knight, " so be it, a-God's
name ! And I will get me gone, with thy
leave, to my lord the king, and will tell
him what thou hast told me. And if thou
wilt give me any word more, now tell it
me." " Yea," said the lady, " tell him
that I send him greeting, and that I can
him much good will for the honour he
biddeth me."

SO the knight departed therewith from
the lady, and came the fourth day
thereafter to King Florus of Ausay, and
found him in his chamber, whereas he was
speaking with his privy counsel. The
knight greeted the king, who returned the
greeting, and made him sit by his side, and
asked tidings of the fair lady, and he told
all her message : how she would not come
to him, whereas she was not his wageling
to come at his command : for that lords
are bound to beseech ladies : how she had
given him word that she sent him greeting,
and could him goodwill for the honour he
bade her. When the King Florus had

heard these words, he fell a-pondering, and spake no word for a great while.
"SIR," said a knight who was of his most privity, "what ponderest thou so much? Forsooth, all these words well befit a good lady and wise to say ; and so, may help me God, she is both wise and valiant. Wherefore I counsel thee in good faith that thou look to a day when thou canst be there ; that thou send greeting to her that thou wilt be there on such day to do her honour, and take her to wife." "Forsooth," said King Florus, "I will send word that I will be there in the month of Paske, and that she apparel her to receive such a man as I be." Then said King Florus to the knight who had been to the lady, that within three days he should go his ways to tell the lady these tidings. So on the third day the knight departed, and went so much that he came to the lady, and said that the king sent word that he would be with her in the month of Paske ; and she answered that it was so by God's will, and that she would speak with her friends, and that she would be arrayed to do his will as the honour of a good lady called on her. After these

words departed the knight, and came to his lord King Florus, and told him the answer of the fair lady, as ye have heard it. So King Florus of Ausay dight his departure, and went his ways with a right great folk to come to the country of the fair lady ; and when he was come thither, he took her and wedded her, and had great joy and great feast thereof. Then he led her into his country where folk made exceeding great joy of her. But King Florus loved her much for her great beauty, and for the great wit and great valiancy that was in her.

AND within the year that he had taken her to wife, she was big with child, and she bore the fruit of her belly so long as right was, and was delivered of a daughter first, and of a son thereafter, who had to name Florence and the daughter had to name Floria. And the child Florence was exceeding fair, and when he was a knight he was the best that knew arms in his time, so that he was chosen to be Emperor of Constantinople. A much valiant man was he, and wrought much wrack and dole on the Saracens. But the daughter became queen of the land of her father, and the son of the King of Hungary took her to wife, and lady she was of two realms.

THIS great honour gave God to the fair lady for the goodness of her and her loyalty. A great while abode King Florus with that fair lady ; and when it pleased God that his time came, he had such goodly knowledge that God had in him a fair soul. Thereafter the lady lived but a half year, and passed away from the world as one good and loyal, and had fair end and good knowledge.

Here endeth the tale of King Florus and the Fair Jehane.

THE HISTORY OF
OVER SEA

I N years bygone was a Count of Ponthieu, *The*
who loved much chivalry and the world, *History of*
and was a much valiant man and a good *Over Sea*
knight.

I N the same times was a Count of St.
Pol, who held all the country, and was
lord thereof, and a man much valiant. He
had no heir of his flesh, whereof he was
sore grieving ; but a sister he had, a much
good dame, and a valiant woman of much
avail, who was Dame of Dontmart in Ponthieu. The said dame had a son, Thibault
by name, who was heir of the country of
St. Pol, but a poor man so long as his uncle
lived ; he was a brave knight and a valiant,
and good at arms : noble he was, and goodly,
and was much honoured and loved of good
folk ; for a high man he was, and gentle of
blood.

N OW the Count of Ponthieu, with
whom beginneth this tale, had a wife,
a much good dame : of the said dame he

had a daughter, much good and of much avail, the which waxed in great beauty and multiplied in much good ; and she was of well sixteen years of age. But within the third year of her birth, her mother died, whereof sore troubled she was and much sorrowful.

THE Count, her father, wedded him right speedily thereafter, and took a high lady and a gentle ; and in a little while the Count had of the said lady a son, whom he loved much. The said son waxed in great worth and in great goodness, and multiplied in great good.

THE Count of Ponthieu, who was a valiant man, saw my lord Thibault of Dontmart, and summoned him, and retained him of his meney; and when he had him of his meney he was much joyous thereat, for the Count multiplied in great good and in great avail by means of him.

AS they returned from a tournament, the Count called to him Messire Thibault, and asked of him and said : " Thibault, as God may help thee, tell me what jewel of my land thou lovest the best?" "Sir," said Messire Thibault, " I am but a poor man, but, as God may help me, of all the jewels

of thy land I love none so much as my
damosel, thy daughter." The Count, when
he heard that, was much merry and joyful in
his heart, and said : "Thibault, I will give
her to thee if she will." "Sir," said he,
"much great thank have thou; God reward
thee."

THEN went the Count to his daughter,
and said to her: "Fair daughter, I have
married thee, save by thee be any hindrance."
"Sir," said she, "unto whom ?" "A-God's
name," said he, "to a much valiant man, of
much avail : to a knight of mine, who hath
to name Thibault of Dontmart." "Ha," sir,
said she, "if thy country were a kingdom,
and should come to me all wholly, forsooth
I should hold me right well wedded in him."
"Daughter," said the Count, "blessed be
thine heart, and the hour wherein thou wert
born."

SO the wedding was done ; the Count of
Ponthieu and the Count of St. Pol
were thereat, and many another good valiant
man. With great joy were they assembled,
in great lordship and in great mirth : and
in great joy dwelt those together for five
years. But it pleased not our Lord Jesus
Christ that they should have an heir of

their flesh, which was a heavy matter to both of them.

ON a night lay Messire Thibault in his bed, and pondered sore, and said : "God ! of whom it cometh that I love so much this dame, and she me, and forsooth no heir of our flesh may we have, whereby God might be served, and good be done to the world." Therewith he thought on my lord St. Jakeme, the apostle of Galicia, who would give to such as crave aright that which by right they crave, and he behight him the road thither in his heart.

THE dame was a-sleeping yet, and when-as she awoke he held her betwixt his arms, and prayed her that she would give him a gift. "Sir," said the dame, "and what gift?" "Dame," said he, "thou shalt wot that when I have it." "Sir," she said, "if I may give it, I will give it, whatso it may be." "Dame," he said, "I crave leave of thee to go to my lord St. Jacque the Apostle, that he may pray our Lord Jesus Christ to give us an heir of our flesh, whereby God may be served in this world, and the Holy Church refreshed." "Sir," said the dame, "the gift is full courteous, and much debonairly will I grant it thee."

I N much great joy were they for long
while : wore one day, and another, and
a third ; and it befell that they lay together
in bed on a night, and then said the dame :
"Sir, I pray and require of thee a gift."
"Dame," said he, "ask, and I will give it,
if give it I may." "Sir," she said, " I
crave leave of thee to go with thee on thy
journey."

W HEN Messire Thibault heard that, he
was much sorrowful, and said : "Dame,
grievous thing would it be to thine heart,
for the way is much longsome, and the
land is much strange and much diverse."
She said : "Sir, doubt thou nought of me,
for of such littlest squire that thou hast,
shalt thou be more hindered than of me."
"Dame," said he, "a-God's name, I grant it
thee."

D AY came, and the tidings ran so far
till the Count of Ponthieu knew it,
and sent for Messire Thibault, and said :
"Thibault, thou art vowed a pilgrim, as they
tell me, and my daughter also?" "Sir," said
he, "that is sooth." "Thibault," said the
Count, "concerning thee it is well, but concerning my daughter it is heavy on me."
"Sir," said Messire Thibault, " I might not

naysay her." "Thibault," said the Count, "bestir ye when ye will; so hasten ye your palfreys, your nags, and your sumpter-beasts; and I will give you pennies and havings enow." "Sir," said Messire Thibault, "great thank I give thee."

SO then they arrayed them, and departed with great joy; and they went so far by their journeys, that they drew nigh to St. Jacque by less than two days.

ON a night they came to a good town, and in the evening Messire Thibault called his host, and asked him concerning the road for the morrow, what road they should find, and what like it might be; and he said to him: "Fair sir, at the going forth from this town ye shall find somewhat of a forest to pass through, and all the day after a good road." Therewith they held their peace, and the bed was apparelled, and they went to rest.

THE morrow was much fair, and the pilgrims rose up at daybreak and made noise. Messire Thibault arose, and found him somewhat heavy, wherefore he called his chamberlain, and said: "Arise now, and do our meyney to truss and go their ways, and thou shalt abide with me and truss our

harness : for I am somewhat heavy and ill The
at ease." So that one commanded the ser- *History of*
geants the pleasure of their lord, and they *Over Sea*
went their ways.

BUT a little while was ere Messire
Thibault and his wife arose and arrayed
them, and got to the road. The chamberlain trussed their bed, and it was not full
day, but much fair weather. They issued
out of the town, they three, without more
company but only God, and drew nigh to
the forest ; and whenas they came thither,
they found two ways, one good, and the
other bad. Then Messire Thibault said to his
chamberlain : "Prick spur now, and come
up with our folk, and bid them abide us,
for ugly thing it is for a dame and a knight
to wend the wild-wood with little company."

SO the chamberlain went his ways speedily ; and Messire Thibault came into
the forest, and came on the sundering ways,
and knew not by which to wend. So he
said : "Dame, by which way go we?" "Sir,"
said she, "by the good way, so please
God."

BUT in this forest were certain strong-
thieves, who wasted the good way, and

made the false way wide and side, and like
unto the other, for to make pilgrims go
astray. So Messire Thibault lighted down,
and looked on the way, and found the false
way bigger and wider than the good ; so he
said: "Come dame, a-God's name, this is it."
So they entered therein, and went a good
quarter of a league, and then began the way
to wax strait, and the boughs to hang alow ;
so he said : "Dame, meseemeth that we go
not well."

WHEN he had so said, he looked before
him, and saw four strong-thieves
armed, upon four big horses, and each one
held spear in hand. And when he beheld
them, he looked behind him, and saw other
four in other fashion armed and arrayed ;
and he said: "Dame, be not abashed at anything thou mayst see now from hencefor-
ward." Then Messire Thibault greeted
those first come, but they held them all
aloof from his greeting. So thereafter
he asked them what was their will toward
him ; and one thereof said : "That same
shall we tell thee anon."

THEREWITH the strong thief came
against Messire Thibault with glaive in
rest, and thought to smite him amidst of

the body ; and Messire Thibault saw the
stroke a-coming, and if he doubted thereof,
no marvel was it ; but he swerved from the
stroke as best he might, and that one missed
him ; and as he passed by him Messire
Thibault threw himself under the glaive,
and took it from the strong thief, and bestirred him against those three whence that
one was come, and smote one of them
amidst the body, and slew him ; and thereafter turned about, and went back, and
smote him who had first come on him
amidst of the body, and slew him.

NOW it pleased God that of the eight
strong-thieves he slew three, and the
other five encompassed him, and slew his
palfrey, so that he fell adown on his back
without any wound to grieve him : he had
neither sword nor any other armour to help
him. So the strong-thieves took his raiment from him, all to his shirt, and his
spurs and shoon ; and then they took a
sword-belt, and bound his hands and his
feet, and cast him into a bramble-bush much
sharp and much rough.

AND when they had thus done, they
came to the Lady, and took from her
her palfrey and all her raiment, right to her

smock ; and she was much fair, and she was weeping tenderly, and much and of great manner was she sorrowful.

THEN one of the strong-thieves beheld her, and said thus to his fellows : "Masters, I have lost my brother in this stour, therefore will I have this Lady in atonement thereof." Another said : "But I also, I have lost my cousin-german ; therefore I claim as much as thou herein : yea, and another such right have I." And even in such wise said the third and the fourth and the fifth ; but at last said one : "In the holding of this Lady ye have no great getting nor gain ; so let us lead her into the forest here, and do our will on her, and then set her on the road again and let her go." So did they even as they had devised, and set her on the road again.

MESSIRE Thibault saw it well, and much sorrowful he was, but nought might he do against it ; nor none ill will had he against the Lady for that which had befallen her ; for he wotted well that it had been perforce and against the will of her. The Lady was much sorrowful, and all ashamed. So Messire Thibault called to her and said : "Dame, for God's sake come

hither and unbind me, and deliver me from
the grief wherein I am ; for these brambles
grieve me sore and anguish me."

SO the Lady went whereas lay Messire Thibault, and espied a sword lying behind there of one of the strong-thieves who had been slain. So she took it, and went toward her lord, full of great ire and evil will of that which was befallen. For she doubted much that he would have her in despite for that he had seen her thus, and that he would reprove her one while and lay before her what had her betid. She said : "Sir, I will deliver thee anon."

THEREWITH she hove up the sword and came to her lord, and thought to smite him amidst of the body ; and when he saw the stroke coming he doubted it much, for he was all naked to his shirt and breeches, and no more. Therefore so hardly he quaked, that the hands and the fingers of him were sundered ; and in such wise she smote him that she but hurt him a little, and sheared the thongs wherewith he was bound ; and when he felt the bonds slacken, he drew to him and brake the thongs, and leapt to his feet, and said: "Dame, so please God, no more to-day shalt thou

slay me." But she said : "Of a surety,
sir, I am heavy thereof."

HE took the sword of her, and put it
back into the scabbard, and thereafter
laid his hand on her shoulder, and brought
her back on the road whereby they had
come. And when he came to the entry of
the wood, there found he a great part of
his company, which was come to meet him ;
and when they saw them thus naked, they
asked of him : "Sir, who hath thus arrayed
you?" But he told them that they had fallen
in with strong-thieves, who had thus en-
snared them. Much great dole they made
thereof ; but speedily were they clad and
arrayed, for they had well enough thereto ;
so they gat to horse and went their ways.

THAT day they rode, and for nought
that had befallen Messire Thibault made
no worser semblance unto the Lady. That
night they came unto a good town, and
there they harboured. Messire Thibault
asked of his host if there were any house of
religion anigh thereto, where one might
leave a lady, and the host said : "Sir, it be-
falleth well to thee ; hard by without is a
house much religious and of much good
dames."

WORE the night, and Messire Thibault
went on the morrow into that house
and heard mass, and thereafter spake to the
abbess, and the convent, and prayed them
that they would guard that Lady there till
his coming back ; and they granted it to
him much willingly. Messire Thibault left
of his meney there to serve the Lady, and
went his ways, and did his pilgrimage the
best he might. And when he had done his
pilgrimage fair and well, he returned, and came
to the Lady. He did good to the house,
and gave thereto of his havings, and took the
Lady unto him again, and led her into his
country with as much great honour as he had
led her away, save the lying a-bed with her.
WHEN he was gotten aback into his
land, much great joy did they make
of him, and of the Lady. At his home-
coming was the Count of Ponthieu, the
father of the Lady, and there also was
the Count of St. Pol, who was uncle unto
my lord Thibault. A many was there of
good folk and valiant at their coming. The
Lady was much honoured of dames and of
damsels.
THAT day the Count of Ponthieu sat,
he and Messire Thibault, they two

131

together, at one dish, and so it fell out that
the Count said to him : " Thibault, fair son,
he who long way wendeth heareth much,
and seeth of adventures, whereof nought they
know who stir not ; tell me tale, then, if it
please thee, of some matter which thou hast
seen, or heard tell of, since ye departed
hence."

MESSIRE Thibault answered him that
he knew of no adventure to tell
of ; but the Count prayed him again, and
tormented him thereto, and held him sore
to tell of some adventure, insomuch that
Messire Thibault answered him : " Sir, since
tell I needs must, I will tell thee ; but so
please thee, let it not be within earshot of
so much folk." The Count answered and
said that it so pleased him well. So after
dinner, whenas they had eaten, the Count
arose and took Messire Thibault by the
hand, and said to him : " Now would I that
thou say thy pleasure, for here is not a
many of folk."

AND Messire Thibault fell to telling
how that it had betid to a knight
and a lady, even as ye have heard in the
tale told ; but he told not the persons
unto whom it had befallen : and the
132

Count, who was much sage and right
thoughtful, asked what the knight had
done with the Lady ; and he answered
that the knight had brought and led the
Lady back to her own country, with as
much great joy and as much great honour
as he had led her thence, save lying in the
bed whereas lay the Lady.

"THIBAULT," said the Count, "otherwise deemed the knight than I had
deemed ; for by the faith which I owe
unto God, and unto thee, whom much I
love, I would have hung the Lady by the
tresses to a tree or to a bush, or by the very
girdle, if none other cord I might find."
" Sir," said Messire Thibault, " nought
so certain is the thing as it will be if the
Lady shall bear witness thereto with her
very body." " Thibault," said the Count,
"knowest thou who was the knight?" "Sir,"
said Messire Thibault, " yet again I pray
thee that thou acquit me of naming the
knight to whom this adventure betid: know
of a verity that in naming him lieth no
great gain." " Thibault," said the Count,
" know that it is not my pleasure that thou
hide it." " Sir," said Thibault, " then will I
tell the same, since I may not be acquitted

thereof, as willingly I would be if it were your pleasure ; for in telling thereof lieth not great avail, nor great honour." "Thibault," said the Count, "since the word has gone so far, know that I would wot straightway who was the knight unto whom this adventure betid ; and I conjure thee, by the faith which thou owest to God and to me, that thou tell me who was the knight, since thou knowest thereof."

"SIR," said Messire Thibault, "by that wherewith thou hast conjured me withal, I will tell thee. And I would well that thou shalt know of a verity that I am the knight unto whom this adventure betid. And wot thou that I was sore grieving and abashed in my heart ; and wot thou well that never erst have I spoken thereof to any man alive ; and, moreover, with a good will had I put aside the telling of it, if it had but pleased thee."

BUT when the Count had heard tell this adventure, much grieving was he, and abashed, and held his peace a great while, and spake no word ; and when he spoke, he said : "Thibault, then to my daughter it was that this adventure betid ?"

"Sir," said he, "of a verity." "Thibault," *The*
said the Count," well shalt thou be *History of*
avenged, since thou hast brought her back *Over Sea*
to me."

AND because of the great ire which the
Count had, he called for his daughter,
and asked of her if that were true which
Messire Thibault had said ; and she asked,
"What?" and he answered : "This, that
thou wouldest have slain him, even as he
hath told it?" "Sir," she said, "yea."
"And wherefore," said the Count, "wouldst
thou have done it?" "Sir," said she,
"hereto, for that yet it grieveth me that I
did it not, and that I slew him not."

SO the Count let all that be, and abode
till the Court was departed. Thereafter was he at Rue-on-Sea, and Messire
Thibault with him, and the son of the
Count ; and the Count let lead with him
the Lady. Then the Count let array a
strong craft and a trim, and did do the
Lady enter therein ; and withal let lay
therein a tun, all new, strong, and great,
and thick. Then they entered into the
said ship, all three, without fellowship of
other folk, save the mariners who rowed
the ship. Then did the Count cause them

to row a full two leagues out to sea ; and much marvelled each one of what he thought to do, but none durst ask him.

BUT when they were so far forth in the sea as ye have heard, the Count let smite out one head of the tun, and took the Lady, who was his daughter, and who was much fair and well attired, and made her to enter in the tun, would she, would she not ; and then let head up the tun again straightway, and dight it well, and let re-do the staves, and stop it well, that the water might not enter in no manner. Then the Count let put it over-board the ship, and he laid hand thereto with his very own body, and thrust the tun into the sea, and said : "I commend thee unto the winds and the waves."

MUCH grieving was Messire Thibault thereat, and the brother of the Lady withal ; yea, and all they that saw the same ; and they fell all at the feet of the Count, and prayed him mercy, that from out of that tun they might take her and deliver her. But the Count, who was much wroth and full of ire, would not grant it them for any thing that they might do or pray. So they let it be, and

136

prayed to Jesus Christ, the Sovereign *The*
Father, that he, of his exceeding great *History of*
goodness, would have pity of her soul, and *Over Sea*
do her pardon of her sins.

THUS have they left the Lady in great
mischief and great peril, even as ye
have heard the tale tell afore, and thus
they returned thence. But our Lord
Jesus Christ, who is the Sovereign Father
of us all, and who willeth not the death of
sinners, be they he or she, but that they
may turn them from their sins and live
(every day he showeth it unto us openly
by works, by examples, and by miracles),
sent succour unto the Lady, even as ye
may hear further on.

FOR the history testifieth us, and telleth
of a verity, that a merchant ship
which came from the parts of Flanders,
before the Count and his fellows were well
come aland, saw the tun floating even as
the winds and waves led it. So said one
of the merchants to his fellows : " Masters,
lo there a tun, and it shall come our way,
meseemeth ; and if we draw it aboard, well
shall we have some avail of it in any case."

NOW know ye that this ship was wont
to go to the Land of the Saracens

for cheaping. So the mariners drew thither where was the tun, and did so much, what by wile, what by force, that they gat the tun on to their ship. And when the tun was laid on their ship, they looked much thereon, and much marvelled . what it might be ; and so much, that they beheld how one of the heads of the said tun was newly arrayed. Wherefore they unheaded it, and found the Lady therein, in such case as though her hour were waning, for air failed her. Her body was big, her visage all swollen, and her eyes ugly and troubled. But when she saw the air, and felt the wind, she sighed a little, and the merchants stood about her and called unto her, but she had no might to speak. But at last the heart came aback to her, and speech withal, and she spoke to the merchants and other folk whom she saw around her ; and much she marvelled when she found herself in such wise amidst of the merchants ; but when she saw of them that they were Christians and mer-chants, the more at ease she was, and much she praised Jesus Christ therefor in her heart, and thanked him of his good-ness, whereas he had so done by her that

138

she yet had a space of life. For she had *The*
much great devotion in her heart, and *History of*
much great desire to amend her life *Over Sea*
toward God, and toward others, of the
misdeeds she had done, whereof she
doubted mightily.

THE merchants asked her of whence
she was, and she hid the matter
from them, and said that a wretched thing
she was, and a poor sinner, even as they
might behold ; and that by much cruel
adventure was she thither come ; and for
God's sake let them have mercy upon her :
and they answered that even so would
they. And she ate and drank, and became
much fair.

NOW so far went the ship of the
merchants, that they came to the
Land of the Saracens, and took haven by
Aumarie. Galleys of the Saracens came to
meet them, and they answered that they
were merchants who led divers merchandise
by many lands; and that they had the
safe-conduct of princes and high barons,
and that they might go into all lands
surely, to seek chaffer and lead their goods.

SO they brought the Lady aland, and
were with her. And one asked the

other what they should do with her ; and one said that they should sell her ; and another said: " If I may be trowed, we shall give her as a gift to the rich Soudan of Aumarie, and then will our matter be mightily amended."

THERETO they accorded all, and they took the Lady and brought her to the Soudan, who was a young man : but first they did do attire and array the Lady much richly, and so gave her to the Soudan, who received the Lady much joyously and with much good-will, for right fair was she. The Soudan asked of them what she was, and they said : " Sir, we wot not ; but by marvellous adventure did we find her."

MUCH good-will had the Soudan to them of this gift, and much good he did to them therefor. Much he loved the Lady withal, and he let serve her honourably. Well was she heeded, and the colour came again unto her, and she became marvellous fair.

THE Soudan fell to coveting the Lady and to loving of her ; and he let ask her by Latiners of what folk she was, but no sooth thereof would she tell him or let

140

him know. Thereof was he heavy, whereas
he saw of her that she was a high woman,
and of gentle lineage. He let ask of her
if she were Christian, and that if she
would leave her law he would take her to
wife, for no wife had he as yet. She saw
well that better it were to come thereto
by love than by force, so she answered that
so would she do of a good will ; and when
she had renied her, and had left her law,
the Soudan took her to wife according to
the manner and wont of the Land of the
Saracens. He held her right dear, and
honoured her much, and waxed of great
love towards her.

BUT a little while was she with the
Soudan ere she was big of a son, and
lay in at her time ; the Soudan was right
glad, and made much great joy. And the
dame was ever of good fellowship with the
folk, and much courteous and of good will
toward them, and learnt so much that she
knew the Saracen tongue.

BUT a little while wore in the years
whereas she had the son, ere she con-
ceived and had a daughter, who anon became much fair and much wise, and in all
lordliness she let nourish her. Thus was

the Lady abiding a two years in much joy
and mirth.

BUT now the story leaves telling of the
Lady and the Soudan till after, as ye
shall come to hear, and returneth to the
Count of Ponthieu, and to the son of the
Count, and to Messire Thibault of Dontmart, who were sore grieving for the Lady
who had been thuswise cast into the sea,
even as ye have heard, and knew no
tidings of her, what was become of her,
and trowed more that she were dead than
alive.

NOW saith the history, and the sooth
beareth witness thereto, that the Count
was in Ponthieu, and his son, and Messire
Thibault. The Count was in sore great
sadness, and heavy thought of his daughter,
and much he doubted him of the sin which
he had done. Messire Thibault durst not
to wed him ; nor did the son of the Count
either, because of the dolour wherein he saw
his friends abiding. Neither would the son
of the Count become knight, though he
were well of an age thereto, had he the
will.

ON a day the Count forthought him
much of the sin which he had done

to his daughter, and he betook him to the *The*
Archbishop of Rheims and confessed to *History of*
him, and said to him all the deed, as he had *Over Sea*
done it. He took the cross of Over Sea,
and crossed him. And whenas Messire
Thibault saw his lord the Count crossed,
he confessed him and crossed him withal.
Likewise, when the son of the Count saw
his father crossed, and Messire Thibault
also, whom he loved much, he also crossed
himself. And when the Count saw his son
crossed, he was much grieved, and said :
"Fair son, wherefore art thou crossed ?
Now shall the land abide void of lord."
But the son answered and said : "Father, I
am crossed for God's sake first before all
things, and for the saving of my soul, and
to serve God and honour him to my power,
so long as I shall have the life in my
body."

SO the Count arrayed him speedily and
bestirred him, and went and took leave ;
but withal he looked to it who should ward
his land. And Messire Thibault and the
son of the Count dight their matters, and
they took to the way with much great safe-
conduct. They came in the Land of Over
Sea safe of body and havings, and there

143

they did their pilgrimage much holily in all the places whereas they wotted that it ought to be done, and God to be served.

AND when the Count had so done, he bethought him that he would well to do yet more : so he gave himself to the service of the Temple for one year, him and his company ; and then when it came to the end of the year, deemed that he would go visit his land and his country. Wherefore he sent unto Acre and let array his journey, and he took leave of them of the Temple, and of the land, and much they thanked him for the honour which he had brought them. He came to Acre with his fellows, and they went aboard ship, and departed from the haven with right good wind at will ; but it endured but for a little ; for when they were on the high sea, then did a wind mighty and horrible fall upon them unawares ; and the mariners knew not whitherward they went, and every hour they looked to be drowned ; and so great was their distress that they bound themselves together, the son to the father, the nephew to the uncle, yea, one to the other, even as they were intermingled. The Count and his son and Messire Thibault

144

bound themselves together so that they
might not sunder.

BUT a little way had they gone in this
wise ere they saw land; and they
asked the mariners what land it was, and
they answered that it was the Land of the
Saracens; and they called it the Land of
Aumarie, and said unto the Count: "Sir,
what is thy pleasure that we do? for if we
go yonder, we shall be all taken and fall into
the hands of the Saracens." The Count said
to them: "Let go according to the will of
Jesus Christ, who shall take heed to our bodies
and our lives; for of an eviller or uglier death
we may not die than to die in this sea."

SO they let run along Aumarie, and galleys and craft of the Saracens came
against them. Wot ye well that this was
an evil meeting; for they took them and
brought them before the Soudan, who was
lord of that land and country. So they
made him a present of the Christians and of
all their havings: the Soudan departed them,
and sent them to divers places of his prisons.
The Count of Ponthieu and his son and
Messire Thibault were so strongly bound
together that they might not be sundered.
The Soudan commanded that they should

be laid in a prison by themselves, where they should have but little to eat and little to drink ; and it was done even as he commanded. There were they a while of time in great misease, and so long that the son of the Count was much sick, insomuch that the Count and Messire Thibault had fear of his dying.

THEREAFTER it fell out that the Soudan held court much mightily, and made great joy for his birthday ; and this was after the custom of the Saracens.

AFTER dinner came the Saracens unto the Soudan, and said to him : "Sir, we require of thee our right." He asked them what it was, and they said : "Sir, a captive Christian to set up at the butts." So he granted it to them whereas it was a matter of nought, and he said to them : "Go ye to the gaol, and take him who has the least of life in him."

TO the gaol they went, and drew out the Count, all bedone with a thick beard ; and when the Soudan saw him in so poor estate, he said to them : "This one hath little might to live ; go ye, lead him hence, and do ye your will on him."

146

THE wife of the Soudan, of whom ye *The* have heard, who was daughter of the *History of* Count, was in the place whereas the Count *Over Sea* who was her father was being led to the death, and so soon as she saw him, the blood and the heart was stirred within her, not so much for that she knew him, but rather that nature constrained her. Then said the Lady to the Soudan : "Sir, I am French, wherefore I would willingly speak to yonder poor man before he dieth, if it please thee." "Yea, dame," said the Soudan, "it pleaseth me well."

SO the Lady came to the Count, and drew him apart, and caused the Saracens to draw aback, and asked him of whence he was, and he said : "Lady, I am of the kingdom of France, of a land which is called Ponthieu."

WHEN the Lady heard that, all the blood of her stirred within her, and straightway she asked of what kindred he was. "Certes, dame," said he, "it may not import to me of what kin I be, for I have suffered so many pains and griefs since I departed, that I love better to die than to live ; but so much can I tell thee of a sooth, that I was the Count of Ponthieu."

WHEN the Lady heard that, she made
no semblance, but forthwith departed from the Count and came to the
Soudan, and said: "Sir, give me this captive,
if it please thee, for he knoweth the chess
and the tables, and fair tales withal, which
shall please thee much ; and he shall play
before thee and learn thee." "Dame," said
the Soudan, "by my law, wot that with a
good will I will give him thee; do with him
as thou wilt."

THEN the Lady took him and sent him
into her chamber, and the jailers went
to seek another, and led out Messire Thibault, who was the husband of the Lady ;
and in sorry raiment was he, for he was
dight with long hair, and had a great beard;
he was lean and fleshless, as one who had
suffered pain and dolour enough. When
the Lady saw him, she said unto the Soudan: "Sir, again with this one would I willingly speak, if it please thee." "Dame," said
the Soudan, "it pleaseth me well." So the
Lady came to Messire Thibault, and asked
him of whence he was, and he said: "I am
of the land of the old warrior whom they
led before thee e'en now: and I had his
daughter to wife ; and I am a knight."

148

THE Lady knew well her lord, so she went back unto the Soudan, and said to him: "Sir, great goodness wilt thou do unto me if thou wilt give me this one also." "Dame, said he," "with a good will I will give him to thee. So she thanked him, and sent him into her chamber with the other.

BUT the archers hastened and came to the Soudan, and said: "Sir, thou doest us wrong, and the day is a-waning." And therewith they went to the gaol and brought out the son of the Count, who was all covered with his hair and dishevelled, as one who had not been washen a while. Young man he was, so that he had not yet a beard; but so lean he was, and so sick and feeble, that scarce might he hold him up. And when the Lady saw him, she had of him much great pity. She came to him and asked of him whose son, and whence he was, and he said he was the son of the first worthy. Then she wotted well that he was her brother, but no semblance she made thereof.

"SIR, certes," said she to the Soudan, "thou wilt now do me great goodness if thou wilt give me this one also; for he knows the chess and the tables, and all other games, which much shall please thee to see and to hear." But the Soudan said: "Dame, by my law, were there an hundred of them I would give them unto thee willingly."

THE Lady thanked him much, and took her brother, and sent him straightway into her chamber. But the folk betook them anew to the gaol, and brought forth another; and the Lady departed thence, whereas she knew him not. So was he led to his martyrdom, and our Lord Jesus Christ received his soul. But the Lady went her ways forthwith; for it pleased her not, the martyrdoms which the Saracens did on the Christians.

SHE came to her chamber wherein were the prisoners, and when they saw her coming, they made as they would rise up, but she made sign to them to hold them still. Then she went close up to them, and made them sign of friendship. And the Count, who was right sage, asked thereon: "Dame, when shall they slay us?" And she answered that it would not be yet. "Dame," said they, "thereof are we heavy; for we have so great hunger, that it lacketh but a little of our hearts departing from us."

THEREAT she went forth and let array meat ; and then she brought it, and gave to each one a little, and a little of drink. And when they had taken it, then had they yet greater hunger than afore. Thuswise she gave them to eat, ten times the day, by little and little ; for she doubted that if they ate all freely, that they would take so much as would grieve them. Wherefore she did them to eat thus attemperly.

THUSWISE did the good dame give them might again ; and they were before her all the first seven days, and the night-tide she did them to lie at their ease ; and she did them do off their evil raiment and let give them good and new. After the eighth day, she had strengthened them little by little and more and more ; and then she let bring them victuals and drink to their contentment, and in such wise that they were so strong that she abandoned to them the victual and the drink withal. They had chequers and tables, and played thereon, and were in all content. The Soudan was ofttimes with them, and good

will he had to see them play, and much it
pleased him. But the dame refrained her
sagely toward them, so that never was one
of them that knew her, neither by word
nor deed of hers.

BUT a little while wore after this matter,
as telleth the tale, ere the Soudan had
to do, for a rich soudan, who marched on
him, laid waste his land, and fell to harry-
ing him. And he, to avenge his trouble,
summoned folk from every part, and
assembled a great host. When the Lady
knew thereof, she came into the chamber
whereas were the prisoners, and she sat
down before them, and spoke to them, and
said : "Lords, ye have told me of your
matters a deal ; now would I wot whether
that which ye have told me be true or not :
for ye told me that thou wert Count of
Ponthieu on the day that thou departedst
therefrom, and that that man had had thy
daughter to wife, and that the other one
was thy son. Now, I am Saracen, and
know the art of astronomy : wherefore I
tell you well, that never were ye so nigh to
a shameful death as now ye be, if ye tell
me not the truth. Thy daughter, whom
this knight had, what became of her?"

"Lady," said the Count, "I trow that she
be dead." "What wise died she?" quoth
she. "Certes, Lady," said the Count, "by
an occasion which she had deserved." "And
what was the occasion?" said the Lady.

THEN the Count fell to tell, sore weeping, how she was wedded, and of the
tarrying, whereby she might not have a
child; and how the good knight promised
his ways to St. Jakeme in Galicia, and how
the Lady besought him that she might go
along with him, and he granted it willingly.
And how they bestirred them with great
joy, and went their ways, and so far that
they came unto a place where they were
without company. Then met they in a
forest robbers well armed, who fell upon
them. The good knight might do nothing
against all them, for he was lacking of
arms; but amidst all that he slew three,
and five were left, who fell upon him and
slew his palfrey, and took the knight and
stripped him to the shirt, and bound him
hand and foot, and cast him into a briar-
bush: and the Lady they stripped, and
took from her her palfrey. They beheld
the Lady, and saw that she was full fair,
and each one would have her. At the last,

they accorded betwixt them hereto, that they should lie with her, and they had their will of her in her despite ; and when they had so done they went their ways, and she abode, much grieving and much sad. The good knight beheld it, and said much sweetly : "Dame, now unbind me my hands, and let us be going." Now she saw a sword, which was of one of the slain strong-thieves ; she took it, and went towards her lord, who lay as aforesaid ; she came in great ire by seeming, and said : "Yea, un-bind thee I will." Then she held the sword all bare, and hove it up, and thought to smite him amidst the body, but by the good mercy of Jesus Christ, and by the valiancy of the knight, he turned upso down, and she smote the bonds he was bound withal, and sundered them, and he leapt up, for as bound and hurt as he was, and said : "Dame, if God will, thou shalt slay me not to-day."

AT this word spake the Lady, the wife of the Soudan : "Ha, sir ! thou sayest the sooth ; and well I know wherefore she would to do it." "Dame," said the Count, "and wherefore ?" "Certes," quoth she for the great shame which had befallen her."

154

WHEN Messire Thibault heard that, *The*
he fell a-weeping much tenderly, and *History of*
said: "Ha, alas ! what fault had she therein *Over Sea*
then, Lady ? So may God give me deliver-
ance from this prison wherein I am, never
should I have made worse semblance to
her therefor, whereas it was maugre her
will."

"SIR," said the Lady, "that she deemed
nought. Now tell me," she said,
"which deem ye the rather, that she be
quick or dead ?" "Dame," said he, "we
wot not." "Well wot I," said the Count,
"of the great pain we have suffered, which
God hath sent us for the sin which I did
against her." "But if it pleased God,"
said the Lady, "that she were alive, and
that ye might have of her true tidings,
what would ye say thereto ?" "Lady,"
said the Count, "then were I gladder than
I should be to be delivered out of this
prison, or to have so much riches as never
had I in my life." "Dame," said Messire
Thibault, "may God give me no joy of
that which I most desire, but I were not
the gladder than to be king of France."
"Dame," said the varlet who was her
brother, "certes none could give me or

promise me thing whereof I should be so
glad as of the life of my sister, who was
so fair a dame, and so good."

BUT when the Lady heard these words,
then was the heart of her softened;
and she praised God, and gave him thanks
therefor, and said to them : " Take heed,
now, that there be no feigning in your
words." And they answered and said that
none there was. Then fell the Lady
a-weeping tenderly, and said to them : " Sir,
now mayest thou well say that thou art my
father, and I thy daughter, even her on
whom thou didest such cruel justice. And
thou, Messire Thibault, thou art my lord
and my baron. And thou, sir varlet, art
my brother."

THEREWITH she told them how
the merchants had found her,
and how they gave her as a gift to the
Soudan. And when they heard that, they
were much glad, and made much great joy,
and humbled them before her; but she
forbade them that they should make any
semblance, and said : " I am Saracen, and
renied, for otherwise I might never endure,
but were presently dead. Wherefore I
pray you and bid you, for as dear as ye

hold your lives and honours, and your *The* havings the greater, that ye never once, *History of* whatso ye may hear or see, make any more *Over Sea* fair semblance unto me, but hold you simply. So leave me to deal therewith. Now shall I tell you wherefore I have uncovered me to you. The Soudan, who is now my lord, goeth presently a-riding; and I know thee well" (said she to Messire Thibault), "that thou art a valiant man and a good knight : therefore I will pray the Soudan to take thee with him ; and then if ever thou wert valiant, now do thou show it, and serve the Soudan so well that he may have no evil to tell of thee."

THEREWITH departed the Lady, and came unto the Soudan, and said : "Sir, one of my prisoners will go with thee, if it please thee." "Dame," said he, "I would not dare trust me to him, lest he do me some treason." "Sir," she said, "in surety mayest thou lead him along ; for I will hold the others." "Dame," said he, "I will lead him with me, since thou counsellest me so, and I will give him a horse much good, and arms, and all that is meet for him."

SO then the Lady went back, and said to Messire Thibault : "I have done so

much with the Soudan, that thou shalt go
with him. Now bethink thee to do well."
But her brother kneeled before her, and
prayed her that she would do so much with
the Soudan that he also should go. But
said she : "I will not do it, the matter
be over open thereby."

THE Soudan arrayed his matters and
went his ways, and Messire Thibault *
with him, and they went against the enemy.
The Soudan delivered to Messire Thibault
arms and horse. By the will of Jesus
Christ, who never forgetteth them who
have in him trust and good faith, Messire
Thibault did so much in arms, that in a
little while the enemy of the Soudan was
brought under, whereof much was the
Soudan rejoiced ; he had the victory, and
led away much folk with him. And so
soon as he was come back, he went to the
Lady, and said : " Dame, by my law, I much
praise thy prisoner, for much well hath he
served me ; and if he will cast aside his law
and take ours, I will give him wide lands,
and richly will I marry him." " Sir," she
said, " I wot not, but I trow not that he will
do it." Therewith they were silent, so that
they spake not more. But the Lady dighted

her business straightway after these things
the best she might, and she came to her
prisoners, and said :

"LORDS, now do ye hold ye wisely, that the Soudan perceive not our counsel ; for, if God please, we shall yet be in France and the land of Ponthieu."

NOW came a day when the Lady moaned much, and complained her, and came before the Soudan, and said : "Sir, I go with child, well I wot it, and am fallen into great infirmity, nor ever since thy departure have I eaten aught wherein was any savour to me." "Dame," said he, "I am heavy of thy sickness, but much joyous that thou art with child. But now command and devise all things that thou deemest might be good for thee, and I will let seek and array them, whatsoever they may cost me."

WHEN the Lady heard that, she had much great joy in her heart ; but never did she show any semblance thereof, save that so much she said : "Sir, my old prisoner hath said to me, that but I be presently upon earth of a right nature, I am but dead and that I may not live long." "Dame," said the Soudan, "nought will I

thy death : look to it, then, on what land
thou wouldest be, and I will let lead
thee thereto." " Sir," she said, " it is of
no matter to me, so that I be out of this
city."

THEN the Soudan let array a ship fair
and stout, and let garnish her well
with wine and victual. " Sir," said the Lady
to the Soudan," I will have with me my old
prisoner and my young one, and they shall
play at the chess and the tables ; and my
son will I take to pleasure me." " Dame,"
said he, "it pleaseth me well that thou do
thy will herein. But what hap with the
third prisoner ? " " Sir," said she, " thou
shalt do thy will herein." " Dame," said
he, I will that thou take him with thee ; for
he is a valiant man, and will heed thee
well on land and sea, if need thou have
thereto."

THEREWITH she prayed leave of
the Soudan, and he granted it, and
much he prayed her to come back speedily.
The ship was apparelled, and they were
alboun ; and they went aboard, and departed from the haven.

GOOD wind they had, and ran much
hard : and the mariners called to

the Lady, and said to her : "Dame, this *The* wind is bringing straight to Brandis ; now *History of* command us thy pleasure to go thither or *Over Sea* elsewhere." And she said to them : "Let run hardily, for I know well how to speak French and other tongues, and I will lead you through all."

NOW so much they ran by day and by night, through the will of Jesus Christ, that they are come to Brandis : there they took harbour in all safety, and lighted down on the shore, and were received with much great joy. The Lady, who was much wise, drew towards the prisoners, and said to them : " Lords, I would that ye call to mind the words and agreements which ye said to me, and I would be now all sure of you, and have good surety of your oaths, and that ye say to me on all that ye hold to be of God if ye will to hold to your behests, which ye have behight me, or not ; for yet have I good might to return."

THEY answered : "Lady, know without doubt that we have covenanted nought with you which shall not be held toward you by us loyally ; and know by our Christendom and our Baptism, and by whatsoever we hold of God, that we will hold to it ; be thou in no doubt thereof."

"AND I will trow in you henceforth," said the Lady. "Now, lords," said she, "lo here my son, whom I had of the Soudan ; what shall we do with him?" "Dame, let him come to great honour and great gladness." "Lords," said the Lady, "much have I misdone against the Soudan, for I have taken from him my body, and his son whom he loved much."

THEN she went back to the mariners, and called and said to them: "Masters, get ye back and tell to the Soudan that I have taken from him my body, and his son whom he loved much, and that I have cast forth from prison my father, my husband, and my brother." And when the mariners heard that, they were much grieving ; but more they might not do ; and they returned, sad and sorrowful for the Lady, and for the youngling, whom they loved much, and for the prisoners, who were thus lost without recoverance.

BUT the Count apparelled himself, whereto he had well enough, by means of merchants and by Templars, who

162

lent him of their good full willingly. *The* And when the Count and his company had *History of* sojourned in the town so long as their *Over Sea* pleasure was, they arrayed them and went their ways thence, and came to Rome. The Count went before the Apostle, and his fellowship with him. Each one confessed him the best that he could ; and when the Apostle heard it, he was much glad, and much great cheer he made of them. He baptized the child, and he was called William. He reconciled the Lady, and set her again in right Christendom, and confirmed the Lady and Messire Thibault, her baron, in right marriage, and joined them together again, and gave penitence to each of them, and absolved them of their sins.

AFTER that, they abode no long while ere they departed from Rome and took their leave of the Apostle, who much had honoured them ; and he gave them his blessing, and commended them to God. So went they in great joy and in great pleasance, and praised God and his mother and the hallows, both carl and quean, and gave thanks for the goods which they had done them.

163

AND so far they journeyed, that they came into the land where they were born, and were received in great procession by the bishops and the abbots, and the people of religion and the other clerks, who much had desired them.

BUT above all other joys made they joy of the Lady who was thus recovered, and who had thus delivered her father, her husband, and her brother from the hands of the Saracens, even as ye have heard. But now leave we of them in this place, and tell we of the mariners who had brought them, and of the Saracens who had come with them.

THE mariners and the Saracens who had brought them to Brandis returned at their speediest ; they had good wind, and ran till they came off Aumarie. They lighted down on shore sad and sorrowful, and went to tell the tidings to the Soudan, who was much sorrowful thereof, and in great dole abode ; and for this adventure the less he loved his daughter, who had abided there, and honoured her the less. Notwithstanding, the damsel became much sage, and waxed in great wit, so that all honoured her and loved

164

her, and prized her for the good deeds
which they told of her.
BUT now the history holds its peace of
the Soudan, who made great dole
for his wife and his prisoners who thus
had escaped, and it returneth to the Count
of Ponthieu, who was received into his
land with great procession, and much
honoured as the lord that he was.

NO long while wore ere his son was
made knight, and great cheer folk
made of him. He was a knight much
worthy and valiant, and much he loved
the worthies, and fair gifts he gave to
poor knights and poor gentle dames of
the country, and much was prized and
loved of poor and of rich. For a worthy
he was, and a good knight, and courteous,
and openhanded, and kind, and nowise
proud. Yet but a little while he lived,
which was great damage, and much was he
bemoaned of all.

AFTER this adventure it befell that the
Count held a great court and a great
feast, and had a many of knights and
other folk with him; and therewithal
came a very noble man and knight, who
was a much high man in Normandy, who

was called my lord Raoul de Preaux. This Raoul had a daughter much fair and much wise. The Count spake so much to my lord Raoul and to his friends, that he made the wedding betwixt William his nephew, son to the Soudan of Aumarie, and the daughter of my lord Raoul, for no heir had he save that daughter. William wedded the damsel, and the wedding was done much richly, and thereafter was the said William lord of Preaux.

LONG time thence was the land in peace and without war : and Messire Thibault was with the Lady, and had of her sithence two man-children, who thereafter were worthies and of great lordship. The son of the Count of Ponthieu, of whom we have told so much good, died but a little thereafter, whereof was made great dole throughout all the land. The Count of St. Pol lived yet, and now were the two sons of my lord Thibault heirs of those two countries, and thereto they attained at the last. The good dame their mother lived in great penitence, and much she did of good deeds and alms ; and Messire Thibault lived as the worthy

which he was, and much did he of good
whiles he was in life.

NOW it befell that the daughter of the Lady, who had abided with the Soudan her father, waxed in great beauty and became much wise, and was called the Fair Caitif, because her mother had left her thus as ye have heard : but a Turk, much valiant, who served the Soudan (Malakin of Baudas was he called), this Malakin saw the damsel to be courteous and sage, and much good had heard tell of her ; wherefore he coveted her in his heart, and came to the Soudan and said to him : "Sir, for the service which I have done thee, give me a gift." "Malakin," said the Soudan, "what gift?" "Sir," said he, "might I dare to say it, because of her highness, whereof I have nought so much as she, say it I would."

THE Soudan, who wise was and clear-seeing, said to him : "Speak in all surety that which thou willest to speak ; for much I love thee and prize thee ; and if the thing be a thing which I may give thee, saving my honour, know verily that thou shalt have it." "Sir," said he, "well I will that thine honour shall be safe, and

against it nought would I ask of thee: but
if it please thee, give me thy daughter, for I
pray her of thee, and right willingly would
I take her."

THE Soudan held his peace and
thought awhile; and he saw well
that Malakin was a worthy, and wise, and
might well come to great honour and
great good, and that well he might be
worthied; so he said: "Malakin, by my
law, thou hast craved me a great thing, for
I love much my daughter, and no heir
else have I, as thou wottest well, and as
sooth is. She is born and come from the
most highest kindred and the most valiant
of France; for her mother is daughter of
the Count of Ponthieu; but whereas thou
art valiant, and much well hast served me,
I will give her to thee with a good will, if she
will grant it." "Sir," said Malakin,
"against her will would I do nothing."

THEN the Soudan let call the damsel,
and she came, and he said to her:
"My fair daughter, I have married thee, if
so it please thee." "Sir," she said, "well is
my pleasure therein, if thou will it." Then
the Soudan took her by the hand, and
said: "Hold, Malakin! I give her to thee."

He received her gladly, and in great joy and in great honour of all his friends; and he wedded her according to the Saracen law; and he led her into his land in great joy and in great honour. The Soudan brought him on his road a great way, with much company of folk, so far as him pleased; then returned, and took leave of his daughter and her lord. But a great part of his folk he sent with her to serve them.

MALAKIN came into his country, and much was he served and honoured, and was received with great joy by all his friends; and they twain lived together long and joyously, and had children together, as the history beareth witness.

OF this dame, who was called the Fair Caitif, was born the mother of the courteous Turk Salahadin, who was so worthy and wise and conquering.

HERE ends the Story of Over Sea, done out of ancient French into English by William Morris.